Presented to

_____

from

_____

_____

Date _____

The
Precious Moments™
Storybook Collection

The PRECIOUS MOMENTS™

Storybook Collection

Stories That Celebrate Everyday Joys

Stories by V. Gilbert Beers

Illustrations by Samuel J. Butcher

An Inspirational Press Book for Children

First Inspirational Press edition published in 1997.

Inspirational Press
A division of BBS Publishing Corporation
386 Park Avenue South
New York, NY 10016

Inspirational Press is a registered trademark of BBS Publishing Corporation

Published for Inspirational Press by Baker Book House, P.O. Box 6287,
Grand Rapids, Michigan 49516.

Library of Congress Catalog Card Number: 97-71142

ISBN: 0-88486-182-1

Printed in the United States of America.

Contents

Through-the-Day Stories

Contents

Letter to Parents

Morning was always a delight for me as a child. In the summer the crowing of a rooster announced the birth of a new day. House wrens joined their voices, along with robins and cardinals. One by one farmyard animals added their sounds, awakening a sleepy world. A symphony had begun, announcing a new day.

These morning songs were graced by the long rays of the sun, streaking across my bedroom window in our old farmhouse. Each ray lit something in my room in a unique way, highlighting that which was usually subdued.

Breakfast scents drifted up from my mother's homespun kitchen—bacon or sausages, eggs, pancakes, or waffles. My mother was not a gourmet cook. We had plain farm cooking. But those smells were ecstasy to a growing boy.

The songs of a new day had begun. The day was mine to enjoy . . . or ignore. I seldom ignored the wonders of each day because each signaled to me some remarkable gift from God.

Wisely, God chose to divide our lives into bite-size chunks called days. Think how oppressive life here on earth would be if it were one long chore for ninety or so years! God was wise also to divide the day into special parts with special interests: morning, noon, evening, night. Each held me captive as a child with its wonderfully unique presentations. Each was mine to enjoy. As you reflect on days gone by, or perhaps even on today, you may feel as I did.

Writing this book has helped me relive the joy of each day. It has reminded me again that the processes of a day are something of great delight if only we will participate in them. I recognize that it was the Creator who made the day, and night, and all variations between.

If this book will stir in your child, and you, a new joy for "the day that God has made," it will have served its purpose.

V. Gilbert Beers

**Who
Wakes Up
the Day?**

Who wakes me in the morning,
  So I can start to play?
  My mother does!
But who wakes up the day?

Who turns the light on in my room,
  So I can have some fun?
  My father does!
But who turns on the sun?

Who starts the water in my bath,
  And closes up the drain?
  My mother does!
But who turns on the rain?

Who fixes things when they don't work,
  When stuff gets cracked or curled?
  My father does!
But who repairs the world?

Who hangs my clothes for me to see,
  Right there before my eyes?
  My mother does!
But who hangs up the skies?

Who wakes the day,
Turns on the sun?

Makes sure the bath
For the world is begun?

Who fixes a world
When it needs repair?
Who hangs the skies,
Away up there?
God does!

Have you thanked your loving mother,
   for getting you up to play?
Have you thanked your loving father,
   for working things out okay?
And have you thanked your heavenly
      Father,
   for waking up the day?

A Day
Is Like
Growing Up

At sunrise the day is a baby

At breakfast, it's a kid like me;

By noon it's like a mom or dad,

And grandparents' time is at three.

At sunset the day is fading
At bedtime we say good-bye;

When stars shine bright,
it's like the time
When we live with God
on high.

**Don't Look
at the Way
Things Look**

"Don't look
    at the way
        things look,"
that's what
    my mother
        will say.

"Don't look
    at what they are
        this morning,
just watch
    how
        they
            change today."

23

A caterpillar is just a caterpillar.
  It can't be a beauty queen.
But things do change and rearrange;
  what you'll see
  is not what you've seen.

A butterfly makes us ooh and sigh,
  as it flies into the sky.
You'd never know how it could grow
  from that wormy little guy.

"Don't look at the way you look,"
that's what my dad will say.
"Don't look in the mirror
and see what you see,
just look at the picture
and see what you'll be."

A barbell is just a barbell.
　You can buy one down at the store.
But if your chest isn't overly blessed,
　you can work up a whole lot more.

"Don't look at the way you look,"
  this birdie
    said to its egg.
"Don't look at your shell
and think you're not well;
  you'll soon fly to Winnipeg."

An egg is just an egg.
  It's not egg-citing today.
But when the shell breaks,
a new life awakes,
  and a beautiful bird soars away.

"Don't look at the way you look,"
  that's what I want to say.
"Don't look in the mirror
and see what you see,
just think of all that you can be."

A kid is just a kid.
  That's what you may want to say.
But the Creator's not done
with what he's begun.
  He will finish a little each day.

A
TICK-TOCK
Time
Rhyme

Why does my clock say
　　TICK
　　TOCK?
The watch on my wrist says
　　TICK
　　TICK.
Shouldn't my clock say
　　TOCK
　　TOCK?
Or would it prefer
　　CLOCK
　　TOCK?

Then should my watch say
    CLICK
    TICK?
Or play a trick and say
    CLICK
    CLICK?

I wonder what makes my
    CLOCK
    TICK.
When time flies fast, does it
    TICK
    QUICK?
Well, this is enough of
    TICKS and
    TOCKS
From tick-tock things like
    WATCHES and
    CLOCKS.
I'm going to stop this
    TICK-TOCK
    RHYME.
Because
  I
    have
      just
        run
          out
            OF
              TIME.

A Breakfast Fit for a King or Queen

"Time for breakfast," Mother called.

Annie and Arnie ran down the stairs. Before Mother could say "hurry," they were sitting at their places at the table.

"What are we having this morning?" Annie asked.

"Surprise," said Mother. "But it's a breakfast fit for a king or queen."

"That's sounds great!" said Arnie. "But what would a king or queen like for breakfast?"

Father smiled when he heard that. "Do you think a king or queen would like waffles?" he asked.

Arnie patted his tummy. "This king would!" he answered.

"So would this queen," said Annie. "Anyone would like waffles!" You've probably guessed that Annie and Arnie both like waffles for breakfast.

"Not anyone," said Father. "Do you remember the horse you rode last summer? He would rather have a bucket of oats for breakfast. I don't think he would like waffles."

"Poor horse," said Annie. "I'd hate to eat a bucket of oats."

"That's because you're Annie," said Mother. "If you were a horse you would love a bucket of oats for breakfast. That's the way God made a horse. And he made Annies and Arnies to like waffles. Different kinds of animals, or people, like different kinds of food."

"Kitty and Puppy sometimes like the same things we do," said Annie.

"Some things," said Mother. "But I think Puppy would rather have dog biscuits than the cherry pie I made for dessert tonight."

"Yuk! I'd hate to eat dog biscuits," said Arnie. "But I LOVE cherry pie."

"I love cherry pie, too," said Annie. "But I would hate to eat that cat food in a can that we give Kitty."

"Let's have a little breakfast guessing

game," said Father. "I'll give an animal and a food. Guess if that animal would like it."

"This sounds like fun," said Annie.

"Would a bunny eat carrots?" Father asked.

"Yes!" Annie and Arnie both shouted.

"But would Kitty eat carrots?" Father asked.

"No!" they both said.

"She might eat cooked carrots," said Father. "But I don't think she would eat raw carrots as a bunny would. Now, would a goldfish like an apple?"

"No," said Annie and Arnie.

"But would Kitty like to eat a goldfish?" asked Father.

Annie and Arnie remembered the time Kitty had tried to catch their goldfish. They were sure Kitty would eat it if she could.

"Would a cow like a hamburger or milkshake?" asked Father.

Annie and Arnie both laughed. That one seemed almost silly.

"Would Annie and Arnie like cotton candy?" Father asked.

"Yes," they both said.

"Do you think a giraffe would like cotton candy?" Father asked.

They were both sure that a giraffe or ele-

phant or rhino or hippo would not like cotton candy.

"But why?" Annie asked.

"God made us to like certain foods so we will eat them," said Father. "He knows what is best for us."

"That's right," said Mother. "A bale of hay would give you a tummy ache. But hamburgers, fries, and shakes might not be very good for a cow, either. God knows what is best for each of us."

"I like candy bars," said Annie. "Does that mean they are best for me?"

"No," said Mother. "Horses like sugar, too. But no one would think of feeding a wonderful horse lots and lots of sugar. Some foods taste good, but we should be careful not to eat too much. God also wants us to learn to say no to things that taste good but aren't good for us."

"I'm glad waffles taste good and are good for us," said Annie.

"Thank you, God, for all good food that tastes good," said Arnie.

Annie and Arnie were very thankful for waffles that morning. They were sure they would not have been as thankful for a bale of hay!

Would you like a bale of hay for breakfast? Be sure to thank God for good food that tastes good.

My Magic Box Down at My Street

There's a magic box down at my street,
You should come and see it,
   it's really neat;
I stuff in a letter, away it goes,
Hopping or skipping on tippy toes.
It finds its way near or far,
To Chattanooga or Zanzibar.
How does it know where it should go
In New York City or Tokyo?
How does it know where to find you,
Does it run down each street
   and avenue?
Does it wear a wonderful thinking cap,
Or strap on a magical radar map?

There's more to this magical box
   that's really neat.
It grabs your letter on Anywhere Street;
And runs through the night,
   looking for me.
I'm sure that's a sight you'd love to see.
By morning mail time its little feet
Have found that box down at my street.
If you'll send a letter, I'll send one, too;
Perhaps we can each say,
   "I love you."

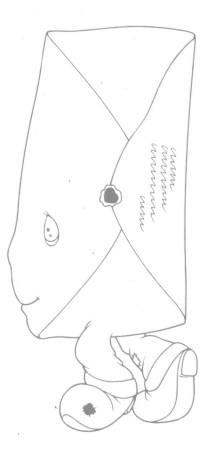

Which Face Are You Wearing Today?

"Ready for school, Mom," Kurt said.

"Good," said Mother. "But which face are you wearing?"

Kurt looked surprised. "I guess I'm wearing the only face I have," he answered.

"Well, there was another boy named Kurt running around the house before," said Mother. "I really couldn't tell who he was. He kept putting on different faces."

"What faces were they?" Kurt asked.

"When this other Kurt got up this morning, he put on his sunshine face," said Mother. "It had a big smile on it. That face

was warm and friendly, like the sun shining."

"I . . . I guess I was glad to get up and get going," said Kurt.

Mother pretended that she didn't hear that the other Kurt was really her Kurt. "Then this Kurt boy couldn't find his shoes," Mother said. "Suddenly he put on a pickle face. You should have seen it! It was long and sour and green, just like a pickle." Mother giggled.

Kurt frowned. He didn't like to think that he had a long, sour green face.

"Oh, yes," Mother went on. "That other Kurt put on a frown face, something like the one you're wearing now. That's because he had to go to school. You should have seen him."

"What other faces did this other Kurt wear?" asked Kurt.

"Let's see," said Mother. "There was a raindrop face. That's when he cried because he had to clean up his room a little. Oh, yes. There was also a pumpkin face. It was like a happy-go-lucky jack-o-lantern face. It really was nice."

"Mom, you do know that I was that other Kurt, don't you?" Kurt asked.

"Oh, my," said Mother. "I'm glad you told me. But you haven't told me which face you will wear to school."

Kurt laughed. "I'll wear my own face," he said. "But I hope it's like the sunshine face."

"It is already!" said Mother. She smiled as she watched Kurt and his sunshiny face run toward school.

By the way . . . which face are you wearing today?

Taking Pictures

Do you have a camera? Do you take pictures? Picture taking is fun. But did you know there are many ways to take pictures?

Casey has a camera. It's just an ordinary camera. It uses ordinary film. It takes ordinary pictures. Casey puts his ordinary pictures in an ordinary photo album. The photos help him remember what he did at school. They help him remember what his family did on special days. They help him remember what his family did on trips. Do you have lots of photos in a photo album?

What kind of pictures are they? What do you remember when you see them?

Casey also has two eyes. He looks at special things. If something is really special, Casey takes a "remember picture" and puts it in his mind. If he wants to remember that special something, he doesn't even look through a photo album. He doesn't turn a page and look for a photo. He just remembers it. He actually sees that "remember picture" as much as he sees a real photo. Do you have lots of "remember pictures" tucked away in your mind? Do you remember them often?

Casey has friends. He has a family. His friends and family watch Casey. When Casey does something special, Mother takes a little "remember picture" of Casey doing that special thing. If Casey does something naughty, a friend at school takes a little "remember picture" of Casey doing that naughty thing. Father takes "remember pictures" of Casey. So do his brother and sister. Many people have hundreds of "remember pictures" of Casey tucked in their minds. They can look at them any time by just remembering them.

God watches Casey every day. He sees everything Casey does. He knows everything Casey thinks. When Casey does good things, God sees every one of them.

God has not only "remember pictures," he even has something like a video tape of Casey's whole life. God's video tape even has pictures of all of Casey's thoughts. Casey squirms when he thinks about that. He would rather forget some of his words. He would rather forget about some things he has done. He would rather not remember some of his thoughts. Do you feel that way, too?

The next time you start to say a bad word, stop! Would you like a photo of you saying that bad word in God's photo album? The next time you start to do something bad, stop! Would you like a photo of you doing that in God's photo album? The next time you think a bad thought, stop! Would you like to see that photo of your thought in God's photo album?

There are many kinds of pictures. You and I should never say, think, or do anything if we wouldn't want to see a picture of it later.

Let's remember that the next time we're tempted to say, think, or do something not-so-good! Let's remember it, too, when we want to do something special.

There's a Mouse in My Lunch!

Did you have a mouse for lunch today? You probably didn't. But Alli did. Mother didn't put it in her lunch box. Alli didn't put it in her lunch box. You might guess that her teacher didn't put it there either.

But someone put a mouse in Alli's lunch box. And the mouse ate big holes in Alli's lunch. Alli wouldn't eat the rest of it.

Who put the mouse in Alli's lunch box? That's what Alli wanted to know.

"I'll get even with him," Alli said. She was sure it was one of the boys who teased her almost every day.

"Do you know who put the mouse in my

lunch box?" Alli asked each of her friends. "I want to get even with him."

She asked Sarah. She asked Amy. She asked Katy. But not one of her friends knew!

"Do you know who put the mouse in my lunch box?" Alli asked some of the boys. "I want to get even with him."

She asked Jason. She asked Jonathan. She asked Kevin. But not one of the boys knew!

Alli sat down at her desk. She began to cry. She was hungry.

Suddenly Alli felt a tap, tap, tap on her

arm. She looked up. Through her very wet tears she saw Sarah and Amy and Katy.

"Let's have lunch," said Katy. "We each want to share some of our lunch with you."

Alli was sure this was the very best lunch she had ever had. And she was sure these were the very best friends she ever had.

"Did you find out who put the mouse in your lunch box?" Sarah asked.

"No," said Alli. "No one will tell me."

"That's because you're asking the wrong question," said Amy. Then she whispered something in Alli's ear. Alli smiled.

Alli was almost through eating her lunch when she saw three boys. They were on the other side of the lunch room. They were watching her. One of them was laughing.

"That's Percival. I think he did it!" Alli whispered. "I'm going to ask him."

"Remember to ask the right question," said Amy.

Alli walked over to the three boys. They looked surprised. They didn't think she would do that.

"Do you know who put the mouse in my lunch box?" she asked sweetly. "I want to PRAY for him."

Percival gulped. The other two boys laughed. They looked at Percival. But Percival wasn't laughing. He looked down at the floor. His friends waited to see what he would do. Suddenly Percival ran out of the lunch room.

Alli put her lunch box on the shelf. She went back to her classroom. She kept thinking of the way Percival looked. She almost felt sorry for him.

After school Alli picked up her lunch box. Then she remembered that she had not thrown the scraps in the garbage.

Alli opened her lunch box. The first thing she saw was a piece of paper with some writing on it.

Alli opened the piece of paper. The writing said:

> I'm really sorry.
> Please forgive me
> and please pray for me
> and my family.
> My mother is sick
> and my father just lost his job.
> Percival.

What do you think Alli did at that very moment? What would you have done?

The Best Restaurant

"We're going out to eat lunch," said Mother. "But where should we go?"

"I want a nice restaurant," said Father. "It must have a beautiful setting with soft music. I want a place that is peaceful."

"And I want a place with great food," said Mother. "It should be the best food in any restaurant anywhere."

"I want a place where we can eat all we want," said Dean. "Some places send you away hungry."

"I want a place with great desserts," said Diane. "Some places just don't have great desserts."

The family began to think of the different restaurants that would have a great setting with soft music, the best food, all you can eat, and great desserts.

The Ritz had a great setting with soft music. But you couldn't eat all you want. Father said he couldn't pay for all Dean wanted to eat.

At The Down and Outers, you could eat all you want, but it didn't have a good setting with soft music.

Another place had good desserts, but not a nice setting. Still another place had great food, but very little for dessert.

Before long Diane and Dean began to argue. Mother and Father wanted to argue, but thought they shouldn't.

"But where can we go with a great setting and soft music, the best food, all you can eat, and great desserts?" asked Mother. "I can't think of a single place."

"Neither can I," said Father.

Mother, Father, Dean, and Diane all sat down and looked sad. Suddenly Dean had an idea. "I know where we can go!" he shouted.

Dean whispered in Diane's ear. Diane smiled. "That's it!" she said. "It has all of these things."

"Well, tell us!" said Mother.

Diane whispered in Mother's ear. "You're right," she said. "That's the only place."

"Looks like I'm the last to know," Father said. "Okay, where is this magic restaurant?"

When Mother whispered in Father's ear, he smiled, too. "Of course!" he said. "It's the only place where you have a great setting and soft music, the best food, all you can eat, and good desserts."

So Mother and Father and Diane and Dean packed the finest picnic lunch you can imagine. They put in lots of great cookies for dessert. And they went to their favorite picnic spot in the woods.

The birds sang. The wind sighed in the trees. The squirrels chattered.

"Best music anywhere," said Father. "And look at this wonderful setting."

"Best food you can buy," said Mother, "even if I did fix it."

"I can eat all I want," said Dean.

"And look at these desserts," said Diane as she munched on a cookie. "But what's the name of this restaurant?"

"I think we should call it Our Family Restaurant," said Dean. So they did!

Can you think of a better name?

Winning and Losing

Would you win a game,
If you lost your best player?

Would you win an argument,
If you lost your best friend?

Would you win a race,
If you lost your sense
    of fairness?

Would you win someone's obedience,
If you lost their love?

Would you win the world's approval,
If you lost your family?

Would you win a promotion,
If you lost your job?

Would you win a battle,
If you lost the war?

Would you win a million dollars,
If you lost your good name?

Would you win the whole world,
If you lost your friendship with Jesus?

Winning something small
May be losing something great.

Winning something great
May be losing something even greater.

Read Matthew 16:26.

I Don't Want to Practice!

"It's not fair! I don't want to practice!" Lucy grumbled. "I just want to play the piano."

Lucy plunked a few notes on the piano. Then she began to daydream.

Lucy pretended that she was in a great hall. There was a beautiful grand piano in the center of the stage. And there were thousands of people in the audience.

These people were dressed up in their best clothes. Lucy smiled as she looked at them. The women wore the most beautiful evening gowns she had ever seen. The men were in tuxedos.

Then Lucy saw the sign. It had her name on it. This was HER great concert.

Lucy stepped out on the stage. The lights in the audience dimmed. Lights shined on her. Lucy bowed. Thousands of people began to cheer and clap. She bowed again. The people jumped to their feet. They clapped and shouted.

"Now this is the way it should be!" Lucy thought. "Who wants to practice when you can have this?"

Lucy walked across the stage. She sat on the piano bench. She was ready.

Suddenly a terrible feeling came over Lucy. What should she play? What could she play? The only thing she knew was the plunk, plunk, plunk piece her teacher had given to her. But she hadn't practiced it yet. She didn't even know plunk, plunk.

Lucy put her hands on the piano. "Plunk, plink, plunk," she played. It sounded terrible. People began to laugh.

Lucy tried again. "Plink, plink, plunk," it went this time. People laughed louder.

Once more Lucy put her hands on the piano keys. Her hands were shaking. Tears came into her eyes. All she could do this time was one little "plunk."

"Booo!" shouted the people. They laughed and laughed. Lucy burst into tears. She ran from the room and locked herself in the bathroom. She cried until she thought her heart would break.

"Is something the matter, dear?" a voice said softly. It was Mother's voice. Then Lucy saw that she was in her own bathroom in her own home.

"I . . . I need to practice," Lucy whispered to Mother.

Mother smiled. "I'm glad to hear you say that," she said. "What happened?"

Then Lucy told Mother about the pretend concert. "It was so beautiful at first," she said. "Then it was awful."

"If it helped you want to practice, it was a great concert," said Mother.

Lucy smiled. Then she bowed and went to her very own piano to practice. There was no one to listen to plunk, plunk, plunk, except her kitty.

Are You Bigger Than a Bee?

If you think that big is better
Than tiny, small, or wee,
Have you ever made a honeycomb
Or ever stung a bee?

When you think you're more terrific
Than a lowly little fly,
Just try to make a mighty leap
A mile into the sky.

If you think that you are tougher
Than an itchy little flea,
Have you ever tried to tickle it,
And make it scratch its knee?

You may not like to hear it,
And perhaps you'll disagree,
But some things are done better by
A fly or flea or bee.

Tigeroo
and
Monkey Two

Said Little Mouse,
   "Come to my house,
We'll nibble on
   some cheese."
"I'd rather nibble
   on a mouse,"
Said Kitty,
   "if
      you
         please."

68

"Come play with me," said Busy Bee,
"We'll fly where it is sunny."
"I'll play with you," said Hungry Bear,
"If I can eat your honey."

"Come play with me," said Tigeroo,
"We'll dance with drum and pipes."
"We'll play with you," said Monkey Two,
"If we can change your stripes."

"Come play with me," said Lonely Jack,
"We'll play with balls and blocks."
"I'll play with you," said Playful Pup,
"But you must leave your box."

"Come play with me," said Woolly Lamb,
"I know you'll be content."
"I'll play with you," said Smelly Skunk,
"But you must wear my scent."

Some friends will play if you will say
And do strange things they do.
But please don't let their different way
Make you a different you.

What Is Play Time?

Do you ever have play time? I do. I'm having my play time now. Mom said so. She told me, "Run outside and play." So, I'm playing. But sometimes I'm not sure that I'm doing what I should do for play time. I'm not even sure what play time is. Do you know?

Do you think play time should be FUN TIME? I guess I have fun most of the time during play time. But sometimes I don't. I think I would have more fun if I had a friend to play with me during play time.

Is that what play time really is? Should play time really be FRIEND TIME? I would

like to play with my friends during play time. But my friends don't live near me. They live too far away to come over for play time. If they played with me, we could do things together. I think that would make play time more fun.

Maybe that's what play time should be! Play time is not just fun time. It's not even just friend time. I guess if I want to have fun with a friend, I must do fun things together with my friend. I guess play time is really TOGETHER TIME. If you could play with me during play time, we could do many things together.

We could make things together.
We could eat together.
We could sing together.
We could ride things together.
We could play games together.
And we could pretend to do fun things.

Do you suppose pretending is what makes play time so much fun together? Do you think play time should really be PRETEND TIME? When we pretend, we can think we're doing many things that we really can't do.

We can pretend we're brave knights fighting in great battles.

We can pretend we're sailing to wonderful places far away.

74

We can
pretend
that we're
grown-ups
like Mom
and Dad.

I asked Mom and Dad what we should pretend if we pretend to be them. Do you know what they said? They said we should pretend that we had a boy like me who

has FUN TIME
during play time,
has FRIEND TIME
during play time,
and TOGETHER TIME
during play time,
and even PRETEND TIME
during play time.

I guess that's what I'll pretend during play time today. I wish you could be with me, my friend, so we could pretend this together and have fun. If you can't, I'll pretend that you're here and that we're having fun pretending to do these things. Is that okay?

Wanda and Wendy

Wanda had a beautiful new puppy. She was so happy. But Wanda had a problem.

"I need a bowl of milk for Puppy," said Wanda. "Where will I find it?"

Wanda looked in her closet. But she could not find a bowl of milk there. She looked in her toy chest. But she could not find a bowl of milk there. She even looked in the refrigerator. But someone had taken all the milk. There wasn't even one drop of milk.

"Poor Puppy," said Wanda. "I must find a bowl of milk for him."

Wendy had a bowl of milk. She was happy with her bowl of milk. But Wendy had a problem.

"I need a puppy to share my bowl of milk," said Wendy. "Where will I find it?"

Wendy looked in her closet. But she could not find a puppy there. She looked in her toy chest. But she could not find a puppy there. She even looked under her bed. But she could not find a puppy there. Do you know why? Wendy did not have a puppy.

Wanda went out to look for a bowl of milk for her puppy.

Wendy went out to look for a puppy for her bowl of milk.

Wanda and Wendy saw each other on the sidewalk.

"Hi, Wendy," said Wanda. "I have a problem. Perhaps you can help me with it."

"Hi, Wanda," said Wendy. "I have a problem, too. Perhaps you can help me with it."

"I have a puppy, but I need a bowl of milk," said Wanda.

Wendy sighed. "I have a bowl of milk, but I need a puppy to drink it," she said.

"Oh, dear," said Wanda. "You really do have a problem. I hope you find a puppy."

"Oh, dear," said Wendy. "You really do have a problem, too. I hope you find a bowl of milk."

Suddenly Wanda looked at Wendy. Wendy looked at Wanda.

"Are you thinking what I'm thinking?" asked Wanda.

"I think I'm thinking what you're thinking," said Wendy. "I am if you're thinking what I'm thinking."

Wendy held out her bowl of milk. Wanda held out her puppy. Now Wanda had a puppy and a bowl of milk. Wendy had a bowl of milk and a puppy.

Soon Puppy had a full tummy.

Wanda and Wendy had a wonderful play time.

Peter the Preacher

"I'm going to be a preacher when I grow up," Peter told Mother.

"Really?" asked Mother. "That would be wonderful. But why do you want to be a preacher?"

"I want to dazzle the crowds," said Peter. "People will sit there and listen to every word I speak. They will sit with their mouths wide open. They will tell each other what a great preacher I am."

"Hmmmm," said Mother. "You may want to think of a better reason to be a preacher."

"Like what?" asked Peter.

"Like helping Jesus do his work," said Mother. "And like helping people find help for their problems in the Bible."

That didn't sound as exciting to Peter as dazzling the crowds. He could see all the people now. There would be thousands of them. They would all sit with their mouths wide open. They could repeat everything he said a week later.

Peter thought he would get started. He found an old orange crate and propped it up in the back yard. He invited some friends to hear him.

Peter's friends sat on the grass in front of him. Peter began to preach. He wasn't sure what he was saying or why he was saying it. But he kept talking anyway.

"Booo," said one of his friends. "Let's go play."

"Stop jabbering," said another. "You're not saying anything. I want a snack."

Peter's friends all walked away. Peter stood there behind his orange crate pulpit. He was alone. This didn't work the way he thought. They were supposed to sit there with their mouths open, listening to everything he said.

Peter found Puppy and Kitty. He plopped them in the grass in front of the orange crate. Peter began to preach.

Puppy sat still for fifteen seconds. But

when Peter shouted, Puppy put his tail between his legs and ran behind some bushes. Kitty ran the other way.

Peter looked at the empty spot on the grass. There weren't thousands of people. There wasn't even one dog or one cat. Nobody wanted to listen to him.

"I . . . I guess I'm a failure," said Peter. "Maybe Mother was right. Maybe I had the wrong reason to preach."

Peter bowed his head. He prayed a little. He asked Jesus to help him have the right reason to preach. But he cried more than he prayed. He felt terrible. He could see thousands of people walking away. Nobody wanted to listen to him. Nobody had mouths open, listening.

Suddenly Peter heard a soft "cheep, cheep" in front of him. He opened his eyes. There was a little bird sitting on his Bible. The little bird looked up at Peter. Peter stared at the little bird.

"I made everyone else come to hear me," said Peter. "But you came all by yourself. You came just when I needed a friend to listen to me."

Suddenly Peter knew that this little bird meant more to him than a hundred people who came but walked away. "Thank you, little bird," he said. "Thank you for coming to hear me."

"Cheep, cheep," said the little bird.
Peter preached softly to the little bird.
This time he didn't pretend that it was an
audience of thousands. He didn't pretend

that they sat there with their mouths open. He pretended that it was one poor person who wanted Jesus to help her. But Peter was so happy. The little bird sat there listening. It even had its mouth open!

"What do you think of my sermon?" Peter asked the little bird when he finished.

"Cheep, cheep," said the little bird.

Peter laughed. "I suppose it is cheap," he said. "I forgot to take the offering. But I feel better anyway. I preached to help Jesus instead of to dazzle the crowds."

That night Peter told Mother about the crowds that went away. He told her about the little bird that said, "Cheep, cheep."

Mother laughed with Peter when he told her that the little bird said his sermon was "cheap, cheap."

"But I learned something very important," Peter told Mother. "I learned that everything I do for Jesus must be to please him and help his people. I must never do his work to dazzle the crowds."

"That lesson didn't cost you a penny," said Mother. "Cheap, cheap!"

Peter and Mother had a good laugh together. Then they went to the kitchen for snack time.

Sailing to All the World

"What are you doing in that old tub?" Father asked.

"I'm sailing away to be a missionary," said Kevi.

"Now?" asked Father.

"Now," said Kevi. "We talked about missionaries in Sunday school this morning. So I'm ready to go right now!"

"Where are you going?" asked Father.

"To all the world," said Kevi.

"It's a big world," said Father. "Are you going to all the world at the same time? Or do you plan to start at one place?"

"I hadn't thought about that," said Kevi. "I

guess I'll start at one place first. How
about Africa?"

"Africa sounds good," said Father. "But
it's also a big place with many countries
and many people. Where are you going in
Africa? You need to decide on one place
there."

"But how will I know which place to
choose?" asked Kevi.

"There are many good ways," said Father.

"Listen to missionaries when they come here. Talk with them. Ask them questions."

"Today?" asked Kevi. "I'm ready to sail, you know."

"You may want to wait," said Father. "Missionaries won't be coming here today. You'll also want to read about the place where you are going. And of course you'll want to talk with the missionary organization that sends you."

"What's a missionary organization?" asked Kevi.

"Some men and women who work together," said Father. "They help missionaries go to the right places to work."

"How do they do that?" asked Kevi.

"First, they make sure you're ready to go," said Father. "They make sure you love Jesus. They make sure you want to tell people that he loves them."

"I love Jesus," said Kevi. "And I want to tell people that he loves them. Maybe I can go today."

"Then they will talk with you about your training," said Father. "Have you gone to Bible school or seminary? Have you had other special training to be a missionary?"

"I can't do all that today, can I?" asked Kevi.

"No, that takes several years after high

school," said Father. "You need to learn many things."

"Why can't I just read my Bible to the people and pray with them?" asked Kevi.

"You can," said Father. "But working as a missionary is much more than that. It's like being a pastor. Our pastor went to school several years after high school."

Kevi was quiet for a moment.

"A missionary organization also helps you get the money you will need," said Father.

"Why will I need money?" asked Kevi. "What will I do with it?"

"You will build buildings and keep them fixed. You will buy Bibles and teaching materials," said Father. "You also need to buy food and clothing for you and your family."

Kevi smiled. It was hard for him to think of having a wife and children.

Kevi jumped from his tub. "Looks like I'd better not sail today," he said. "I've got a lot of work to do first. While I'm working, I can tell my friends and neighbors about Jesus."

"First things first," said Father. "Now it sounds like the very first thing is dinner. I hear Mother calling."

"Let's go!" said Kevi. "All this travel has made me hungry."

Holly's Hotline

"What did you do at school today, Holly?" her dad asked at dinner.

"We talked about hotlines in one of my classes," Holly answered. "I guess you have to be a very important person to have a special phone like that."

"Usually presidents and prime ministers have hotlines," said Dad. "That's so they can talk with each other about very important things."

"Do we have a hotline?" Holly asked.

Dad laughed. "Our line seems hot when you talk too long on the phone," he said.

"But it's not really a hotline. We don't need a hotline."

"Why?" asked Holly. "Don't we have important things to talk about?"

"Yes, we hope all that we say is important," said Dad. "But we don't talk with presidents and prime ministers, so we don't need a special phone."

Holly was quiet for a long time. Dad thought she was almost too quiet.

"But Dad," said Holly at last, "we talk with God about things. So why don't we have a hotline to him?"

Now Dad was quiet for a while. "I guess we do," he said. "It's called prayer. We don't need a phone to talk with God. He hears us without a phone."

"Even if we have something important to say to him?" Holly asked.

"Yes, even if we have something very important," said Dad.

That night when she was alone, Holly thought about school. She thought about the girl who made fun of her. She thought about hurting her finger at recess. She thought about not doing well when the teacher asked her to recite. She thought about spilling some juice on her good dress. Then a tear came into her eye.

Holly looked at the phone. "Maybe our phone really is a hotline to God," she said.

"Maybe no one really tried to call God on our phone."

Holly picked up the phone. She wasn't sure about God's phone number. Then she saw the letters with each number.

"I know what I'll do," said Holly. She touched 4. That had a G next to it. She touched 6. That had an O next to it. And then she touched 3. That had a D next to it.

"See, that spells GOD," said Holly.

Holly listened for God to answer. But it was quiet at the other end. Holly was sure that God was listening, so she began to tell him about her day.

"Do you think God listened on our hotline?" Holly asked Dad later. She told him what she had done.

"I'm sure he listened," said Dad. "He listens to all his important people. And you are one of his very important people."

"Just think!" said Holly. "A president or prime minister only has a hotline to another president or prime minister. But I have a hotline to God!"

"Makes you pretty special," said Dad.

**A Nap
Is Not
for Nat
(Me!)**

I have a hundred reasons why
A nap is not for Nat.
The afternoon was made for play.
Who wants to snooze away the day?
A nap is for a cat!

My mother wants me napping, but
A nap is not for Nat.
My toys get lonely when I'm gone.
They start to cry when I first yawn.
A nap is for a cat!

I wish my mother understood,
A nap is not for Nat.

I'll need at least a dozen drinks.
"That's thirteen times too much!" she
    thinks.
A nap is for a cat!

I think my mother is unfair,
A nap is not for Nat.
A thousand friends will come to play,
While I must sleep the day away.
A nap is for a cat!

I guess I must stop thinking that
        A nap is not for Nat.
        Because I heard what Mother said,
            "Stop arguing and get to bed!!!"
                So . . . I'll catnap
                    with my cat!

My
Pet
Parade

My mom will let me get a pet,
But I'm not sure which pet to get.

A hairy ape
  will help me
    scare
Those scary kids
  who shout,
    "I dare!"

94

But when I need a pocket, too,
I'll wish I had a kangaroo.

A cow will mow my grass for me,

Giraffes will
help me
climb a tree.

96

A frog will feast
 on flies and fleas,

ZAP!

A mouse will
 air-condition cheese.

A lion will guard my door at night,
A bird will help me fly my kite.

I'd like a rhino
on my team,

A unicorn will
share ice
cream.

But wait!

There's something I've not thought of yet!
If I'm not there, who'll feed my pet?

A
New
Friend

There was no one as sad
as Grandpa McPhatt,
When he lost his pet pussy,
a fat tabby cat.

But down at the pet shop
a fellow named Ace
Said he'd find a pet kitty
to take tabby's place.

There were
Angora,
Abyssinian,
Malay,
and Maltese,

Almost any conceivable cat
    that you'd please.
But Grandpa kept thinking
    about his one special cat,
No pedigreed Persian
    could ever top that.

So he left the pet store
    at the heart of the mall,
And he came back home
    with no cat at all.
He was feeling alone,
    with no one to share
His home and his food
    and his soft easy chair.

Then suddenly from somewhere a small
    face appeared,
A soft little fellow, long-tailed and pink-
    eared.
Then Grandpa decided there's a place in
    his house

For his new little friend
    who's a wee little
    mouse.

Now Grandpa
    McPhatt
    learned what you
    know, too,
That it's tough to lose
    someone
    precious to you.
And when someone's
    no longer
    there in your house,
You'll be glad for a
    friend,
        perhaps
            even
            a
                mouse.

Pet
Time

Cats
and
Dogs

Mother says my brother and I fight like cats and dogs. But I guess I didn't know how cats and dogs fight. So I decided to watch Kitty and Puppy.

The other night I stayed up late to watch how Kitty and Puppy fight when I go to bed. I thought they would put on little boxing gloves. I wanted to see if they fight that way. But they didn't fight at all. Puppy opened an eye once and looked at Kitty when she yawned. I think he wanted to be sure she was okay. Kitty yawned once. She opened one eye and looked at Puppy. I guess she wanted to be sure he was okay, too. Maybe I should watch my brother more to be sure he's okay.

This morning I accidentally stepped on Puppy's tail. He yelped a little yelp and crawled into the corner. Kitty went over and rubbed against him. I think she was purring. Do you think she wanted to make him feel better? Maybe I should help my brother feel better each time he gets hurt.

When I came home from school, my brother and I played ball. Kitty and Puppy played ball with us, too. My brother and I argued a couple of times. We even said some things brothers and sisters shouldn't say to each other. But Kitty and Puppy didn't argue. They didn't say one mean word to each other. Maybe my brother and I should watch how Kitty and Puppy play. Maybe we could learn some good things from them.

This afternoon I talked with Mother. I told

her what I had learned from Kitty and Puppy. Mother smiled and said she could be wrong. Maybe my brother and I don't fight like cats and dogs. Maybe we fight like brothers and sisters. And maybe, just maybe, we could learn some more good things from Kitty and Puppy.

**Are
Birthday Pets
Like
Birthday
Kids?**

Someone
    came into
        my pet shop
            today.
She wanted
    a special pet
        for her
            one-year-old.
"What kind of pet?"
    I asked.
"Oh, almost any kind will do,"
    she said.

"But it must be **soft and cuddly.**
One-year-olds are **soft and cuddly**,
   you know."
Do you know one-year-olds who are
   soft and cuddly?
   Who are they?
Do you know animals who are
   soft and cuddly, too?
   What are they?

Someone came into my pet shop today.
He wanted a special pet for his two-year-
old.
"What kind of pet?" I asked.
"Oh, almost any kind will do," he said.
"But it must be **bouncy.**
Two-year-olds are **bouncy,** you know."
Do you know two-year-olds who are
bouncy?
Who are they?
Do you know some animals who are
bouncy, too?
What are they?

Someone came into my pet shop today.
She wanted a special pet for her three-
    year-old.
"What kind of pet?" I asked.
"Oh, almost any kind will do," she said.
    "But it must like to **squeal and get dirty.**
    Three-year-olds like to
        squeal and get dirty, you know."
Do you know three-year-olds who like to
    squeal and get dirty?
    Who are they?
Do you know some animals who like to
    squeal and get dirty, too?
    What are they?

Pet
Time

Do
Angels
Have Pets?

Do angels have pets?
I hope that they do.
But are angel pets
Purple, orange, or
blue?

Do angel pets fly?
  Can they hop, skip, or walk?
And do angel pets
  Really know how to talk?

Does an angel pet sleep
  In a basket or bed?
And what is its name,
  Angelina or Fred?

Do angel pet choirs
  Like to bark, chirp, or sing?
Does an angel pet have
  At least one little wing?

Does an angel lamb *baa-aah*
  Or an angel cat *mee-ow?*
Does an angel-like pup
  Say an angel *bow-wow?*

Is angel food cake
  An angel pet treat?
I wonder what angel pets
  Really would eat.

Do angels have pets?
  I hope that they do.
If I were an angel,
  I would. Would you?

Chore
Time

Angel Chores

"It's not fair!" Gretchen grumbled. "I don't have any time to play. All day long I'm doing nothing but chores."

Mother smiled. "All day long?" she asked. "Poor Gretchen! You must be so tired. I do hope you have a little strength left. I really need that thread."

Gretchen smiled a little smile. She knew that Mother had not asked her to do one other thing all day long. That was her only chore so far. But she had a bad habit of grumbling when Mother asked her to do any chore. You could even call her Grumbly Gretchen.

Gretchen gave the thread to Mother. Then she sat down to play with her doll again. "There must be someone who doesn't have chores," she grumbled again. Then Gretchen saw a Sunday school paper lying on the sofa. It had a picture of an angel on it.

"Angels don't have chores," she complained. "I wish I were an angel."

Mother smiled. "Sometimes you are my little angel," she said. "But not when you grumble about chores. Anyway, how do you know that angels don't have chores?"

"Do they?" asked Gretchen.

"I don't know," said Mother. "But what if God asked angels to do some special chores for him? Do you think they would grumble?"

Gretchen giggled. She didn't think angels would grumble about anything. "What kind of chores would God ask an angel to do?" she asked.

"I don't know," said Mother. "But let's pretend:

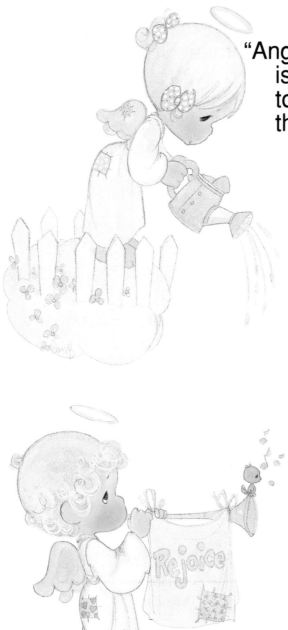

"Angela Angel
is sprinkling the earth
to make
the flowers grow.

"Andrew Angel
is tooting his trumpet
so the morning sunrise
will glow.

"Allan Angel
    brings in the rainbow
    after the
    morning rain.

"Aaron Angel
    gets rid of things
    that people
    won't need again."

"I guess I wouldn't grumble if God asked me to do those things," said Gretchen.

"Because the chores are fun or because you love God?" Mother asked.

"Because I love God," said Gretchen. "So I guess I shouldn't grumble about your chores either, because I love you."

Gretchen really tried to stop grumbling about the few chores Mother asked her to do. Oh, she probably forgot and grumbled once in a while. But, whenever she thought about the angel chores, she tried not to grumble.

So, will you remember not to grumble, whenever you think of the angel chores?

Saving
Time

My
Piggy

Sarah was a spender. She liked to spend every penny someone gave her. She also liked to spend every penny she earned. Sarah couldn't wait to spend it for something special. She spent her money as soon as she got it.

"Why don't you save some of your money," said Mother. "When you get enough, you can spend it for something special."

Sarah tried that two or three times. But every time she looked at her money, she wanted to spend it.

"I have an idea," said Mother. "Why not

spend some of your money for a piggy bank? You can save your money in it. You won't see it. So you won't want to spend it."

Sarah thought that was a good idea. So she spent some money for a piggy bank. Mother helped her buy it. Sarah thought it was the cutest little piggy in all the world.

It was fun to save money in this cute piggy bank. Each time Sarah put money into the piggy, she talked to it. She pretended the piggy could hear her.

"You're helping me save my money, you know," Sarah told the piggy one day.

"You're the cutest piggy I've ever seen," Sarah told the piggy another day.

"I like having you in my room," Sarah told the piggy still another day.

Each day Sarah talked to her piggy bank. Each time she put money into it, she told it how cute it was, or how much she liked it.

Each day Sarah told her mother how much she liked this cute piggy bank. At first she called it "that piggy bank." Then she called it "my piggy bank." Then she began to call it "My Piggy!"

Sarah saved every penny she earned. She saved every penny someone gave her. That's so she could talk to Piggy when she put money into him. Saving was such fun now.

One day Sarah went to Amy's birthday party. You should see the beautiful doll Amy got for her birthday! Sarah wanted a doll like that. She was sure that she must have enough in Piggy to buy her doll.

After Amy's birthday party, Sarah ran home as fast as she could. She found a hammer and ran to her room. She would smash that piggy bank and get the money for the doll.

Then Sarah looked at her piggy bank. It wasn't "that piggy bank." It was "My Piggy." A tear came to Sarah's eyes. She was almost sure that she saw a tear in Piggy's eyes, too.

Sarah put the hammer away. "I won't smash Piggy for any old doll," she said.

The next day Sarah went to Sunday school. The teacher told Sarah and her class about a missionary family their church supported. They had a little girl Sarah's age. Their house had just burned. They lost everything they had. If people didn't help them, they would have to come home. They would have to stop working for Jesus in that place until they could get a new house.

"We're going to take an offering next Sunday," said the teacher. "If you want to help Jesus do his work, this is a good place to give some of your money."

On the way home, Sarah thought about this missionary family. She thought about the girl her age.

"I want to give the money I have in My Piggy," she said. "That's much more important than buying a doll."

When she came home, Sarah got the hammer again. She would simply HAVE to break Piggy open for Jesus.

But when Sarah looked at her Piggy she began to cry. Piggy had a tear, too.

But Sarah lifted the hammer. "I MUST get my money out for Jesus," she said. Sarah lifted the hammer three times. Each time she said, "I MUST get my money out for Jesus." But each time she put the hammer down. She could not break her Piggy.

Sarah ran to Mother as fast as she could go. She was crying so much she thought her heart would break.

"What should I do?" she begged.

"About what?" asked Mother.

Sarah told Mother about wanting to give her money to Jesus. She was even willing to break her Piggy for Jesus. But it was SO hard to do it.

"That's easy," said Mother. "Why don't you use the key that came with the bank? Or did I forget to tell you about the key?"

Sarah stared at Mother. She threw her arms around Mother and cried some more.

"Oh, thank you, thank you, thank you," Sarah said. She probably said "thank you" a dozen times.

If you ever want to see a happy Sarah, you should have seen Sarah opening Piggy's tummy with the key Mother gave her. Sarah had a smile as big as the sun. She was sure that Piggy had a smile just as big, too.

King Kent of Kent's Kingdom

Kent liked to play after he came home from school. Sometimes he liked to play outside. Sometimes he liked to play inside. On rainy days he liked to play inside more than outside. Do you?

On this rainy day Kent sat down with his crayons, scissors, paper, and glue. He began to cut and color and glue.

"You're so busy," said Mother. "What are you making?"

"I'm making a surprise," said Kent. "You'll be proud of me when you see it."

"I'm always proud of you," said Mother. "But this sounds quite special."

"Oh, it is!" said Kent. "When I finish this, I will be a very important person."

"It sounds like a very important activity," said Mother. "I can hardly wait to see it."

Kent was busy for a long time. At last he called for Mother.

"Come and see my surprise," he said.

Mother hurried to see Kent's surprise. There was Kent, still holding his scissors and glue. Crayons stuck out of his back pocket with his sling. Paper and crayons were all over the floor.

But, most important, Kent wore a big smile. He also wore a paper crown he had made.

"I'm a king!" said Kent. "I'm King Kent of Kent's Kingdom!"

"That's exciting," said Mother. "You will make a good king. But what do you want to do as king?"

Kent was quiet for a moment. "Do kings have to do something?" he asked. "I thought they were just kings."

Mother said, "Good kings do good things. Bad kings do bad things. But they all do some things."

"I want good things in my kingdom," said Kent. "Kent's Kingdom will be a good place. But can't I just BE good? Do I have to DO good things?"

Mother smiled. "When you're good, you

do good things," she said. "When you do good things, you show that you are good."

"Then I guess I want to BE good and DO good things," said King Kent. "Is wearing a crown doing something good? Must I do something more?"

"A king isn't a king because he wears a crown," said Mother. "A king wears a crown because he is first a king. If you want to be a king, you must do things good kings do."

"Like what?" asked King Kent.

"Kingly kindness is a good start," said Mother. "Do kind things for your subjects."

King Kent laughed. "Who are my sub-jects?" he asked.

"How about Kitty and Puppy?" asked Mother.

"I'll do kind things for them," said King Kent. "I'll love them, too."

"That's fit for a king," said Mother. "A good king should love his subjects. And he will help take care of his subjects."

"Sounds like I have some royal work to do," said King Kent. "It is time to feed Kitty and Puppy. So I'll wear my crown while I feed my subjects."

"When you're through, you can join us for a palace banquet," said Mother. "Din-ner is almost ready. But do kings help their mothers wash and dry dishes after the palace banquet?"

"This king will," said Kent. "I'll even wear my crown. Helping my mother is kingly work, you know!"

Wouldn't you like to have a picture of King Kent wearing his crown while he helped mother with the dishes? Father took one. He might show it to you some time.

What's
for
Dinner?

Are chocolate eggs
   for
     breakfast,

Or
cornflakes
  made
   for
    lunch?

Do most of us
   start out the day
With birthday cake
   and punch?

Would Puppy like a cherry pie,
And would you want his bone?
Would you enjoy a piggy's grain,
And he your ice-cream cone?

Would Teddy Bear sit in a chair
And feast on candy cane?
And would a cow begin right now
A diet of chow mein?

Is lemonade that's freshly made
The thing for every critter?
And would you pay to buy some hay
For baby's baby-sitter?

You wouldn't be exactly glad
For dinner at the zoo.
So you'll be glad to know that God
Has planned good foods for you.

The Queen of Clean

When it was time for Doreene to help with the dishes, she began to complain. "Why do we have to rinse and wash and scrub and dry all these old dishes?" she moaned.

When Mother asked Doreene to help dust the furniture, she griped about that. When it was Doreene's time to clean her room, she had a few things to say about that, too.

When it was time to help mother wash the clothes, Doreene grumbled about that. "Just think," she said, "if we wore all these

clothes twice as long before washing, we would wash half as much."

"Your math is great," said Father. "But the Queen of Clean wouldn't rule a kingdom like that!"

"Who is she?" Doreene asked. She had a little half-smile when she asked. She knew Father would tell a story, which he did. This is Father's story:

Once upon a time, the Countess of Complaining complained about almost everything. That's why she was the Countess of Complaining. But she complained most about washing and drying dishes, washing clothes, keeping her room clean, and dusting the furniture.

One day the Countess of Complaining had a big royal party. She invited all her favorite royal guests.

The Duke of Dust arrived first. He came as soon as the Countess complained about dusting furniture. The Duke had a big bag of dust with him. He sprinkled it over all the furniture in the palace.

The Countess didn't care. "Someone else will clean it up," she thought. She never thought about who that "someone else" would be.

The Duchess of Dirty Dishes arrived next. She came as soon as the Countess complained about rinsing, washing, and drying dirty dishes. You should have seen all the dirty dishes the Duchess had with her.

The Countess was sure that the Duchess must have had a banquet of garbage. These were not just dirty dishes. They were yukky, sticky, gooey, dirty dishes. Even the pigs would have been ashamed of them! The Duchess piled all her dirty dishes in the sink. They reached to the ceiling of the palace. Mustard, ketchup, syrup, and leftovers dripped from the dishes.

The Countess didn't care. "Someone else will clean it up," she thought. She never thought about who that "someone else" would be.

The Marquis of Mud was next. He came when the Countess complained that she always had to take off her muddy shoes at the door. Of course the Marquis didn't do that. He had so much mud on his shoes that he could hardly walk. He took a tour of the palace. There was a mile of mud everywhere.

The Countess didn't care. "Someone else will clean it up," she thought. She never thought about who that "someone else" would be.

Prince Pig Sty came next. He arrived when the Countess complained about washing and ironing clothes. His clothes looked as if he had just come from a long game of football with the pigs. They were filthy. The Countess was sure he had not washed his clothes in a month of Sundays. When he came in, Prince Pig Sty sat in every pretty chair he could find. He loved to see the dirty streaks that he left behind.

The Countess didn't care. "Someone else will clean it up," she thought. She never thought about who that "someone else" would be.

Baron La Mold left moldy pieces of bread in the corners of the palace. General Germs coughed and sneezed at everyone he could find. Admiral Hornblower left a trail of dirty tissues on the floor. Major Mess threw toys and junk everywhere.

The Countess didn't care. "Someone else will clean it up," she thought. She never thought about who that "someone else" would be.

At last the party was over. The royal guests all went home. The Countess went to bed and slept very well because she was sure that "someone else will clean up all the mess" while she slept.

But the next morning the Countess was surprised. Dirty food still dripped from the dishes. Dust still covered all the furniture. There was still a mile of mud throughout the palace. Everywhere she looked she saw dirty tissues, toys, and junk. No one else had cleaned it up.

Suddenly the Countess remembered. In real life, Mother cleaned up these things when she complained and didn't help. But Mother didn't live in this Pretend Palace!

Eight hundred and eighty-eight days later, the Countess was just cleaning up the last of the mess. Suddenly there was a knock on the door. When she opened the door, there were all her royal friends—the Duke of Dust, the Duchess of Dirty Dishes, the Marquis of Mud, Baron La Mold, Prince Pig Sty, General Germs, Admiral Hornblower, and Major Mess. They wanted another party.

"Go away and never come back," said the Countess. "You're not wanted!"

"But you always wanted us before," they said.

"That's when I was the Countess of Complaining," she said. "Now I'm the Queen of Clean. From now on, I want to have the cleanest castle in the kingdom."

When Father finished his story, Doreene smiled. "I guess I want to be the Queen of Clean instead of the Countess of Complaining," she said. "Doreene, the Queen of Clean! That sounds good. I think Mother will like to hear my new title."

From that time on, whenever Doreene thought about complaining, she remembered the royal guests and the eight hundred and eighty-eight days of cleaning up their mess. Whenever there was anything to be cleaned, Doreene became Mother's special helper.

"The Queen of Clean at your service!" she would always say with a smile. Then the Queen of Clean and Mother would have a mess cleaned up in less than eight hundred and eighty-eight seconds!

Moving Day

Moving day, please go away,
And don't come back another day.
I really do not want to go
To a strange home that I don't know.
I fear my friendships all will end,
And I'll go there without a friend.

I'm filled with fear, I cry at night,
I'm scared that things won't work out
    right.
I really do not want to go
To a strange home that I don't know.
I fear my friendships all will end,
And I'll go there without a friend.

I'll leave friends here who care for me,
But will I find new friends friendly?
I really do not want to go
To a strange home that I don't know.
I fear my friendships all will end,
And I'll go there without a friend.

Will kids at school refuse to play?
Will they have nasty things to say?
I really do not want to go
To a strange home that I don't know.
I fear my friendships all will end,
And I'll go there without a friend.

But then last night I learned in prayer
My Best Friend is already there.

Moving day, don't go away,
I'm ready now, please come today.
I know I'm ready now to go
To that strange home that I don't know.
I've learned new friendships all begin
Not with new kids, but from within!

Because last night I learned in prayer
My Best Friend is already there.

What's So Special About a Baby?

What's so special about a baby?

A baby
can't say
one word
can't wash
one dish
can't feed
one pet

But a baby is very, very special. Why?

Is it because a baby
doesn't say one mean word,
doesn't break one dish, or
doesn't tease one pet?
No, that's not what makes a baby special.

What's so special about a baby?

A baby
can't cook one meal
can't play ball
can't ride a bike

But a baby is very, very special. Why?

Is it because a baby
doesn't burn the toast,
doesn't throw a ball through the window,
   or
doesn't fall from a bike and skin her
   knee?
No, that's not what makes a baby special.

What's so special about a baby?

A baby
can't drive a car
can't play with brothers and sisters
can't climb stairs

But a baby is very, very special. Why?

Is it because a baby
doesn't get a speeding ticket,
doesn't fight with brothers and sisters,
  or
doesn't fall down stairs?
No, that's not what makes a baby
  special.

If a baby doesn't give us trouble
  because he can't get into trouble,
And doesn't argue
  because she can't talk,

And doesn't go to bad places
   because he can't walk,
And doesn't fall
   because she can't stand up,
Does that make a baby special?
No, these are not the things that make a
      baby special.

What's so special about a baby?
A baby is very, very special because:

   When I see our newborn baby,
      I remember our Creator.
   When I see our baby's smile,
      I remember God is love.
   When I see how helpless baby is,
      I remember God's watchcare.
   When I see our baby's little feet,
      I remember to follow Jesus.
   When I see our baby's tiny fingers,
      I remember the joy of serving Jesus.
   When I see our baby's soft lips,
      I remember to tell others about Jesus.
   When I hear our baby coo,
      I remember to praise our Lord.
   When I see our baby's softness,
      I remember God's compassion.
   When I see our baby drinking milk,
      I remember God provides.
   When I see our baby in our arms,
      I remember God holds us tight.

When I see our baby awake each morn-
   ing,
   I remember God was with me through
   the night.
When I see our baby go to sleep,
   I remember God is with us always.
When I see our baby grow,
   I remember God is faithful.

Thank you, Lord, for showing us more
   about you,
   as we see our little baby.

Take a Bow

"How did you like Diane's piano recital, Denny?" Mother asked.

"It was okay," said Denny. "She did a good job with her piece. But why did people clap for the piano players? Why did the piano players bow when they did?"

"When Father and I go to musical concerts, people clap for the musicians there, too," said Mother. "Then the musicians bow. Sometimes the people clap for a long time."

"Why?" asked Denny.

"We clap because we like what they did

for us," said Mother. "We clap to say 'thank you.' They bow to say 'you're welcome.'"

"But you don't clap for me when I do something special," said Denny. "If you did, I'd take a bow, too!"

"Would you like that?" said Mother.

"That would be fun!" said Denny.

"We'll talk about it when Father comes home," said Mother.

Father smiled when Denny told him about clapping and taking a bow. Father and Mother said they would try it. Diane thought it was silly.

Denny was so happy to hear this. At last his family would show they appreciated him.

But Denny had almost forgotten about their little talk when he and Diane fed Puppy and Kitty. When they finished, Mother and Father clapped and cheered for Denny.

"Take a bow, Denny," said Father.

Denny bowed. He felt a little silly, though. After all, he had just done his chores.

"Wait a minute!" said Diane. "I fed Puppy and Kitty, too."

"We'll clap for you, if you want us to," said Father.

"I'd feel absolutely stupid," said Diane. "Feeding Puppy and Kitty is part of our chores. Don't clap for me."

As soon as Denny and Diane had helped Mother set the table, Mother and Father clapped their hands.

"Yeah, Denny!" they shouted. Father even gave a long whistle.

"Diane helped, too," he said, sheepishly.

"She doesn't want us to clap for her, Denny," said Father. "Take a bow."

Denny gave a little halfhearted bow. He wasn't so sure this really was fun. He really did feel silly.

After dinner, Mother and Father jumped up from the table. They began to clap and cheer for Denny.

"What's that for?" asked Denny. "I didn't do anything."

"You ate dinner," said Mother. "Yeah, Denny. Take a bow."

Denny started to get up from the table to take a bow. But he couldn't do it.

"I feel stupid!" he said. "I don't want clapping for eating dinner."

"How about for helping with dishes?" asked Mother. "Or cleaning up your room or going to school or getting good grades?"

"I don't want you to clap for me for any of these things," said Denny. "I *should* go to school, get good grades, clean up my room, feed our pets, help set the table, and eat my dinner."

"Then what should we clap for?" asked Mother.

"Nothing," said Denny. "But I do want to take a bow." So Denny bowed.

"What for?" asked Father.

"That's my way of saying 'thank you' to my parents for all they do for me," he said. "I never clap for all the things you do for me, so I'll take a bow."

Would you like to clap your hands or take a bow to your parents for all they do for you? Or would you rather just say "thanks"?

Full Heart and Empty Bank

Penny was sad. She wanted to buy something special for each person in her family. But she had no money. Her piggy bank was empty.

"I wish I could buy that beautiful dress for Mother," said Penny. "But I don't have one dollar." Penny shook her piggy bank. There wasn't one dollar in it.

"I wish I could buy that sweater Father wants," said Penny. "But I don't have one quarter." Penny shook her piggy bank. There wasn't one quarter in it.

"I wish I could buy that beautiful doll for my little sister," said Penny. "But I don't

have one nickel." Penny shook her piggy
bank. There wasn't one nickel in it.
"I wish I could buy that beautiful bike for
my big brother," said Penny. "But I don't

have one dime." Penny shook her piggy bank. There wasn't one dime in it.

Penny shook her piggy bank again. She knew what she would hear. There was nothing in it, not even one penny. She wished she could hear even one little penny rattling around inside. But she didn't. It was empty.

Poor Penny! Her heart was full, but her bank was empty.

Penny sighed.

Then Penny had an idea. "I can't BUY each of my family members something special," she said. "But maybe I can DO something special for each one."

Penny ran to find Mother. She was getting ready to wash the dinner dishes.

"Mother, Mother," said Penny, "I have a wonderful gift for you."

Mother smiled. She knew that Penny did not have even one penny to buy a wonderful gift.

"I'm going to wash and dry all the dinner dishes," said Penny. "And you are going to sit down and read."

Mother smiled. "All by yourself?" asked Mother. "Are you sure?"

Penny looked so happy that Mother knew she was sure.

When Penny finished the dishes, she ran

to find Father. He was getting ready to sweep the garage.

"Guess what!" said Penny. "I have a wonderful gift for you."

Father smiled. He knew that Penny did not have even one penny to buy a wonderful gift.

"I'm going to sweep the garage for you," said Penny. "And you are going to sit down and read."

Father smiled. "All by yourself?" he asked. "Are you sure?"

Penny looked so happy that Father knew she was sure.

When Penny finished sweeping the garage, she ran to find her big brother. He was getting ready to feed Puppy and Kitty.

"Guess what?" said Penny. "I have a wonderful gift for you."

Penny's big brother smiled. He knew that Penny did not have even one penny to buy a wonderful gift.

"I'm going to feed Puppy and Kitty for you," said Penny. "And you are going to play with your toys."

Penny's big brother smiled. "All by yourself?" he asked. "Are you sure?"

Penny looked so happy that her big brother knew she was sure.

When Penny finished feeding Puppy and

Kitty, she ran to find her little sister. She was getting ready to play all by herself.

"Guess what?" said Penny. "I have a wonderful gift for you."

Penny's little sister smiled. She knew that Penny did not have even one penny to buy a wonderful gift.

"I'm going to play with you," said Penny.

"Are you sure?" asked Penny's little sister. She knew that it wasn't much fun for big sisters to play little-sister stuff with their little sisters.

Penny looked so happy that her little sister knew she was sure.

Later that evening, Penny walked into the living room. There were four smiling people, waiting for her.

"Guess what!" said Penny's little sister.

"We have a wonderful gift for you," said Penny's big brother.

"A big hug," said Father.

"For a wonderful girl," said Mother.

So Penny had four big hugs, one from Mother, one from Father, one from her big brother, and one from her little sister.

Penny didn't even bother to shake her empty piggy bank. She thought she was the richest girl in all the world.

What do you think?

Mike
the
Knight

"Who is this fierce-looking knight?" asked Father.

"I'm Mike the Mighty Knight," said Mike.

Mike the Knight looked something like a real knight. He had a sword, a helmet, and a shield. He pretended that his shirt was armor.

"I'm ready to fight," said Mike.

"Whom do you want to fight?" asked Dad.

"I want to fight those guys at school who made fun of me," said Mike.

"I'm sorry they did that," said Father. "Why did they make fun of you?"

"Because I told them that I love Jesus,"

said Mike. "And because I told them that I read my Bible and pray. They also want me to do some things that would not please Jesus."

Father smiled. "Mike the Knight, there are some people like that where I work," he said. "They make fun of me because I love Jesus. They tease me because I read my Bible and pray. They think I should do some of the bad things they do."

"After I fight those guys at school, I'll come and fight those guys at your work," said Mike.

Father smiled. "With your sword?" he asked. "What do you want to do to your guys and my guys?"

"I'll chop them with my sword," said Mike.

"That's sounds rough," said Father. "Do you really want to hurt them?"

Mike hadn't thought about that. He really didn't want to hurt anyone with his sword. He just wanted to stop the teasing. He didn't want to do the bad things his friends did. But he didn't want to chop anyone either.

"You need a different sword to fight your friends," said Father.

"But this is a genuine, trusty, guaranteed knight's sword," said Mike. "It's the best!"

"I'm sure it's the best sword to hurt people," said Father. "But you're not going to

win your battle for Jesus by chopping people with that kind of sword. There is a special sword to help you win Jesus' battles."

Mike looked puzzled. "Can I buy one?" he asked. "Does it cost a lot of money?"

"You already have one," said Father.

"I do?" asked Mike. He really looked puzzled now. "What is it? Where is it?"

"Come with me, Mike the Mighty Knight," said Father. Mike and Father went to Mike's room. Father picked up Mike's Bible.

"Here it is!" said Father.

"But . . . but that's not a sword," said Mike. "That's just my Bible."

"It doesn't look like a sword," said Father. "But it is."

Father opened Mike's Bible and read from Ephesians 6:11–17.

"Put on the whole armor of God," Father read. Then Father read about God's special sword, his Word, the Bible.

"Does the Bible really say that?" asked Mike the Knight. "Does the Bible really say that it is God's special sword?"

"Yes, it does," said Father. "Ordinary knights wear ordinary swords. They chop people with them. But Christians are God's special knights. We use God's special sword, the Bible, to help Jesus."

Mike the Knight put down his knight's

sword. He picked up God's sword, his Bible.

"I'm ready to change swords," he said. "But how do I use it as a sword?"

"You don't chop people with it," said Father. "You share it with others, the way Jesus did when he was tempted."

Father read the story in Matthew 4:1–11 about the devil tempting Jesus. "Every time the devil tempted Jesus, he answered him with a Bible verse," said Father. "Each Bible verse was like a sword jabbing the devil. But God does the jabbing, we don't!"

"So when my friends tempt me to do something wrong, I should share a Bible verse with them?" asked Mike the Knight.

"Try it!" said Father. "That's what I do with my friends at work. It works."

"I will," said Mike. "I want to have my sword ready, so I'm going to start memorizing some Bible verses."

Would you like to get your sword ready, too?

Why Do I Say No?

When Mother knows what's good for me,
  Why do I say no?
When Father says, "This way is best,"
  Why don't I want to go?

When teacher tries to help me learn,
  Why do I refuse?
When choosing chores will help me grow,
  Why don't I choose to choose?

When Jesus walks ahead of me,
  And gives me all I need,
Or when he wants to guide my life,
  Why don't I let him lead?

I think I know what I should do,
  When tempted to say no.
I'll ask the Lord what he would do,
  And that's the way I'll go.

What Should I Say to God?

"Bedtime, Barry!" Mother called.

"That means it's time to pray," said Barry. "Why do I have to pray every night before I go to bed?"

"You don't have to," said Mother. "But don't you want to?"

"I guess so," said Barry. "But sometimes I don't know what to say to God."

Mother smiled. "Most people wonder what they should say to God," she said. "They're afraid they aren't saying the right words."

"I guess I should just keep asking him for

things," said Barry. "Isn't that what we should do when we pray?"

"You can ask him for what you want," said Mother. "Or you can ask him for what is best for you."

Barry thought about that. "I . . . I guess I've really been asking for what I want," he said. "Maybe some of these things aren't so good for me. Maybe God really doesn't want me to have every one of them."

"I'm glad to hear you say that," said Mother. "Many of my friends haven't figured that out yet. They pray, 'Dear God, gimme what I want.' That's a GIMME PRAYER."

Barry laughed. "What kinds of prayers should I pray?" he asked.

"Let's start with a THANK-YOU PRAYER," said Mother. "Thank God for good things he has given you."

"I could pray an hour about that," said Barry. "What else?"

"How about a PRAISE-YOU PRAYER?" said Mother. "Tell God how glad you are for the kind of person God is. Praise him for his love. Praise him for his kindness. Praise him for His goodness. You could think of a dozen good things about God."

"I guess I could pray an hour about that, too," said Barry. "Is there another kind of prayer I should remember?"

"I don't have to tell you much about a HELP-ME PRAYER," said Mother. "When you need help, I know you will ask God to help you. But how about an I-GIVE-YOU PRAYER? You can talk with God about what you will give Him."

Barry was quiet when Mother said that. "I guess I'm always asking God for so much I never tell him what I want to give him," he said. "I want to give him some of my money. But what else?"

"You can sing well," said Mother. "That's called a talent. You can give that to God. So now you have two things—money and talents. But what is the most important gift you can give God?"

Barry smiled. "I know!" he said. "I can give him myself."

"God would rather have that special gift than all the money you could give," she said.

"Prayer time," said Barry. "I have lots and lots of things to pray about tonight."

What Do You Want?

If God would give
   you anything,
What would
   you ask today?
If God would share
   while you're at prayer,
What would
   you want to pray?

Would you become a movie star,
  Or quarterback a team?
Would you request a pirate chest,
  A truckload of ice cream?

A castle might be very nice,
  A red sports car or two.
What if God made a great parade,
  Or a circus just for you?

A million dollars would be great,
  A million more is greater.
How about the gold to fill the hold,
  Of a twenty-mile-long freighter?

If you could be the smartest kid,
  You'd know that you would pass.
You'd spend all day at fun and play,
  And still be first in class.

If God would give you anything,
  Would these things pass the test?
Or could he pour out something more,
  To help you have his best?

I'd think you'd give up anything,
  To know that God loves you.
So when you pray, perhaps you'll say,
  You'll give him your love, too.

**I
Don't
Know
Why**

I don't know why it happens,
  When I reach out for a crown,
When I think
    that I deserve
    the prize,
The world
    turns
      upside
        down.

173

I don't know why it happens,
When I think that I am best,
When I think that I can prove it,
Something puts me to the test.

I don't know why it happens,
  When I think I'm very wise,
And I think I know the answer,
  Something cuts me down to size.

I don't know why it happens,
  When I'm proud of what I've done,
And I want to show off all my works,
  That I'm forced to show off none.

Wait! I do know why it happens!
  I remember it today!
I find that things don't turn out right,
  When I forget to pray!

A Little Lamb Whispered

A little lamb whispered
  softly today,
"Please be my shepherd,
  show me your way.
But before you lead,
  I hope that you go,
Where
  your
    Shepherd
    leads
  and
   helps
    you
     to
      grow."

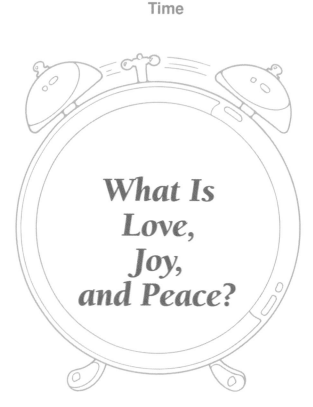

What Is Love, Joy, and Peace?

What is love?
Do you know?

My mother says,
"It's
  changing
    dirty
      diapers
And
  scrubbing
    dirty
      toes.

It's working hard without reward."
Do you suppose she knows?

What is joy?
Do you know?

My mother says,
"It's more than being happy,
By getting lots of things.
It's the deep-down satisfaction
That serving Jesus brings."

What is peace?
Do you know?

My mother says,
"It's more than being quiet,
Away from girls and boys.
It's pleasing God and building kids,
With lots of family noise."

Bath
Time

Connie's Complaints

"Why do I have to look so ugly with these old curlers tonight?" asked Connie.

"So you can look beautiful without them tomorrow," said Mother.

"Why can't I look beautiful without them tonight *and* tomorrow?" asked Connie.

"Does your hair curl all by itself?" Mother asked.

"No," said Connie.

"Do you want to get up early so I can curl it with a curling iron in the morning?"

"No."

"Do you want to go to school with your hair not curled?"

SCALES

"No."

"Do you know some other way to curl your hair?"

Connie thought a while. She didn't know of any other way to have curly hair. And she did want curly hair.

"Why didn't you let me eat that candy tonight?" Connie grumbled.

Mother smiled.

"How many pieces did I let you eat?" she asked.

"Two."

"How many did you want to eat?"

"Hundreds."

"How much do you think you and I would weigh if we ate hundreds of pieces of candy?"

Connie frowned. She didn't even want to think about that.

"Why do I always have to take a bath with that old soapy water," Connie complained.

"So you will keep clean," said Mother. "If you don't keep clean, you can get germs. Your friends may also sit on the other side of the room."

This time Connie smiled. She knew what Mother meant. But Connie was on a roll with her complaints.

"Why do I have to scrub my pretty teeth with that old toothbrush?" Connie groaned.

"So your pretty white teeth won't get yellow fur all over them," said Mother. "You don't want to see yellow fur all over your teeth, do you?"

"Yuk!" said Connie.

"Also, if you don't brush your teeth, they get cavities easily," said Mother. "Do you like it when the dentist drills holes in your teeth to fill them?"

"Ouch!" said Connie.

But Connie was still grumbling and complaining about curlers, candy, soap, and toothbrushes when she went to sleep. It just didn't seem fair that she had to mess around with all those things.

That night Connie dreamed a strange dream. She threw all her curlers, bath soap, and toothbrushes in the garbage. She was so happy to throw all that junk away. She wouldn't have to mess with those things any more.

Then Connie sat down with the biggest

box of chocolates that you've ever seen. It was as big as her bed. She ate and ate and ate. She ate the whole thing!

You would think that Connie would brush her teeth after eating so many chocolates. But she didn't. And she didn't take a soapy bath or curl her hair either.

In her dream Connie saw herself getting bigger and bigger. She had to run from her room so she could get through her bedroom door. When she looked in the mirror in the hallway, she looked like a big Connie-shaped balloon. Then she saw that her hair was long and stringy. She looked at her teeth. They had yellow fur on them.

Connie dreamed that she was suddenly at school. But her friends laughed at her because she was a Connie-shaped balloon with stringy hair and yellow furry teeth.

Her friends also sat on the other side of the room because she hadn't bathed with soapy water. Connie began to cry. She was ashamed to be a Connie-shaped balloon with stringy hair and furry yellow teeth. She was ashamed that kids wanted to sit on the other side of the room.

Connie cried all the way home. She tried to get into the house, but she couldn't get through the door. Connie pounded on the door and screamed for Mother.

Suddenly Connie felt a warm hand touch her forehead. "Bad dream?" a soft voice asked.

Connie looked up. She was in her bed in her room. Mother was smiling at her. She wasn't a big Connie-shaped balloon with stringy hair and yellow furry teeth. She was little. Her teeth still felt minty from brushing. But she did have curlers in her hair.

"I'm glad for curlers and toothbrushes and toothpaste and soapy bathwater," Connie whispered to Mother. "And I'm glad you didn't let me eat all the candy I wanted."

"I'm glad that you're glad," said Mother. "And I know you'll still be glad in the morning." And she was!

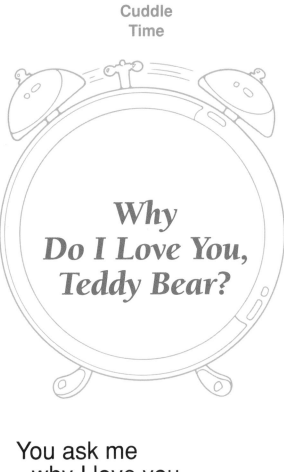

Why Do I Love You, Teddy Bear?

You ask me
  why I love you,
  Teddy Bear?
I'll tell you
  if you promise not to tell
  anyone else.
Okay?

I love you
  because you never
  argue or fight with me.
You'll never do that,
  will you?

I love you
　　because you never say
　　mean things about me
　　to your friends.
I wish I could say that
　　about my
　　other friends.

I love you
　　because you're always there
　　when I need a friend.
You always will be,
　　won't you?

I love you
  because you always smile
  at me.
You'll never frown
  or look angry at me,
  will you?

I love you
  because you've never
  run away from me.
You'll always be there with me,
  won't you?

I love you
  because you're huggable.
When I need someone to hug,
  you comfort me.

I love you
  because you watch over me
  all night while I'm asleep.
You never close your eyes when
  I close mine.

I love you
  because you're always
  the same.
You're not in a good mood one day
and a mean mood the next.
  I can always
  count on you being the way
  you are.

I love you
  because you keep on
  loving me,
  even when I say mean things.
Even if I were naughty,
  you would still
  love me.

I love you
  because you make me happy.
I feel a warm fuzzy feeling when
  I'm with you.

And do you know what,
Teddy Bear,
I guess I love God because
He never argues or fights with me.
He never says mean things about me.
He's always there when I need a friend.
He always seems to have a smile
for me,
at least when I'm good.
He never runs away, he's always there.
He's lovable and huggable.
He watches over me all night while
I'm asleep.
He's always the same.
He keeps on loving me, even when I'm
not lovable.
He makes me happy
and gives me
wonderful warm feelings
when he's with me.
He does many, many more
wonderful things
that a little Teddy Bear
can't do.

Thank you,
Teddy Bear,
for being so
wonderful.
That's why
I love you.

Thank you,
dear God,
  for being
  much, much
    more wonderful.

That's why I love you
  much, much more
  than even my wonderful
  Teddy Bear.

That Million-Dollar Something

There's a million-dollar something
 that I am looking for.
It's worth at least a million,
 or maybe even more.

It's something that you cannot find
 in any super store.
But that million-dollar something
 makes you want a million more.

You can't stuff that million something
 in your pocket, purse or shoe.
It's something you can't wash or wear,
 it's something you can't chew.

That million-dollar something
  makes you feel that you're brand-new.
I especially want this something
  if it comes to me from you.

You must not miss that marvelous thing
  and feel you're really smug.
It's worth too much to rent or buy
  in bag or box or jug.

That million-dollar something
  is as snuggly as a rug,
because, my darling Mommy dear,
  it's your million-dollar hug!

The Tear Wiper

Dawn and her dad always had a little talk before bed time. Dawn usually told Dad the good things that happened that day, and the not-so-good things, too.

"I fell down when I was roller skating," said Dawn. "It really hurt! I cried a little."

"I'm sorry you hurt," said Dad. "If Mother or I had been there, we would have given you a big hug."

"Some kids made fun of me at school this morning," Dawn said. "I cried even more than when I fell."

"That's a different kind of hurt," said Dad.

"Hurting our hearts can be more painful than hurting our bodies."

"Then, on the way home from school, that big dog down the street came out and barked at me," Dawn added. "I was so scared. I cried then, too."

Dad thought a minute or two. "Mother and I can't be there to hug you every time you get hurt," he said. "We would if we could, but we can't."

"I know that," said Dawn. "But I wish someone could hug me each time I cry."

"You need a Tear Wiper," said Dad.

"What's a Tear Wiper?" asked Dawn.

"Someone to wipe away your tears when you cry." said Dad. "You need someone to comfort you and make you feel better when you hurt."

"Do you mean someone I could carry in my pocket?" asked Dawn. "He would have to be very small. Are there mice-like Tear Wipers?"

"Pretend ones, perhaps," said Dad. "But there is a better one than that."

Dawn looked puzzled. "What is it?" she asked. "Who is it?"

"There's a Tear Wiper who is always with you," said Dad.

"There is?" asked Dawn. "Where? Who?"

"Each time you get hurt, he will make you feel better if you ask him," Dad added.

"I want to ask him," said Dawn. "But who is he?"

"His name is Jesus," said Dad. "You can't carry him in your pocket. You don't need to. But he always goes with you. Next time you get hurt, ask him to comfort you. Ask him to be your Tear Wiper."

"I will, I will," said Dawn.

So Dawn prayed to her Tear Wiper right then. And she asked Jesus to wipe away her tears for that day. She asked Jesus to comfort her. Do you think he did?

Why Do I Sleep?

"Time for bed," said Mom. "Dad and I will come and tuck you in."

"Why do I have to go to bed?" asked Rita. "Why do I have to sleep, anyway?"

"I've wondered that, too," said Dad. "Sometimes we wish we could just keep on playing or reading or talking. Why sleep?"

"Well, why do we sleep?" asked Rita. "Why can't I stay up all night?"

"Want to try?" asked Dad. He had seen Rita yawn three times on the way to her bedroom.

Rita yawned again. "Some other night,"

she said with a smile. Rita knew that she would not stay awake very long.

"But why do I sleep?" Rita asked again.

Dad smiled this time. "I guess you deserve an answer," he said. "You have asked three times. Rita, I don't know all that happens to us while we sleep. We dream, and God must help us do that for a good reason. I think there are a lot of other good things that happen while we sleep. We don't even know some. Now, let's pretend."

"Let's pretend that I start our car and run it full speed all day. Then I never turn it off. I keep it running fast all night and all the next day. It just keeps on running full speed, day after day. What do you think will happen to that car?"

"I think that poor car might wear out fast," said Rita. "Or it might get tired and crash."

"I think so, too," said Dad. "Let's pretend again."

"Let's pretend that you're a cowgirl, riding on a fast horse. Because he's fast, you make him keep running as fast as he can all day and all night and all the next day. That poor horse never stops. He just keeps running at full speed. What do you think will happen to that horse?"

"I think that poor horse might fall over and die," said Rita.

"I think so, too," said Dad. "Horses must rest like cars and kids. But let's pretend once more."

"Let's pretend that there is a dear little girl named Rita. She likes to run and play. Because she likes to do that, she keeps on running and playing all day. Then she keeps on all night and all the next day. She never stops running and playing. What do you think will happen to that dear little girl?"

"I think she will wear out fast," said Rita. "She may even crash like the car."

"I think so, too," said Dad. "Kids must rest like cars and horses. So God gives us sleep to help us turn off our tired bodies and minds. It's like turning off the car lights. The battery lasts longer!"

Rita yawned. "Are you through?" she asked. "I'm tired. I want to go to sleep."

"Good night, Rita," said Dad.

"Good night, Rita," said Mom.

"Good niii . . . . . zzzzz," said Rita.

Through-the-Year Stories

Contents

Letter to Parents

Growing up on an Illinois grain farm offered me a carousel of the four seasons, and a smorgasbord of all that went with them. Farm life meant outdoor life much of the time and that meant participating with autumn leaves, shocks of corn, thunderstorms, falling snow-flakes, frosty designs on the old farmhouse windows, the first buds on the trees in the spring, summer gardening, and hundreds of other signs of the wonders of God's special through-the-year fingerprints and footprints on our world.

The seasons and their unique wonders meant so much to me, and to my wife, Arlie, that they became the focal point of many of our activities with our five growing children. Some of our happiest memories with our chil-dren are those associated with the wind blowing in the trees, discovering wildflowers in the woods, finding animal shapes in puffy white summer clouds, building snowmen, and raking autumn leaves. Seasonal pictures always found their places around our house, hanging on walls, adorning the refrigerator door and almost any place the children could hang them. Is it surprising that our grandchildren are now enjoying these same wonders?

With the advent of television many of our children are losing their appreciation for God's created wonders. If this book serves as an appetizer for you and your children to participate in seasonal wonders, it will have served you well. But while you find affinity with your children and creation, I trust also that you, and they, will find affinity with the Creator.

V. Gilbert Beers

January

Something New

There's something new
    around our house;
It's not a cat,
    it's not a mouse.

It's nothing that
    my mother hid,
So don't try lifting
    every lid.

And Dad says, "No,
    I didn't hide
A thing for you
    to find outside."

Oh, now I think I'm very near!
I found we have a *BRAND NEW YEAR!*

January

Betty B. wants to be
Outside skating with you and me.

Christopher C. wants to see
How fast his sled slides when it's slippery.

Donna D. wants to be free
To help Mom take down
the Christmas tree.

Everett E. said to me,
"I'd rather say HAPPY NEW YEAR
To the other three."

My Snowfriend

Suppose you and I could make a very best friend. We might make this friend from boards or bricks or gadgets or widgets. Or we might even make this friend from snow. That's it! We'll make a snowfriend.

What kind of friend should we make? What kind of friend would be just right for us? Have you ever thought about this?

I want a friend who is bigger and meaner than any other kid on the block. No one will bully this new friend. If I need someone to chase away kids that pick on me, I will tell my bigger and meaner friend. He will certainly not let those kids pick on me. He will teach them a lesson they will not forget.

What did you say? This is not such a good idea? What if my bigger and meaner friend is not always friendly with me? What if he helps the other big kids pick on me?

I suppose you're right. No, we must not make a bigger and meaner friend. He may not be a good friend at all.

You say you want a friend who has lots of other friends. She is very popular. Everyone likes this friend. Whenever the kids choose teammates for a game, she is the first one chosen. Whenever we have a school play, she gets the best part. She's pretty and smart, the very best girl on the block.

But listen to what I am saying. This is not such a good idea! If she is that popular, she may not spend much time with you. If you ask her to come over to play, she may say, "I'm sorry, you will have to make an appointment. The only time I have left is next Tuesday at four in the afternoon."

You think I'm right? Of course I am. No, we must not make a very popular friend like that. She may not be a good friend at all.

How would you like a friend who has lots and lots of money? Whenever we want an ice cream cone, he will buy it for us. Whenever we want to go to the candy store or circus, he will have the money to take us. Don't you think that's a good idea?

You don't? What are you saying? You think we might ask our friend for too many things? I suppose you are right. If we think of money all the time, we'll stop thinking of all the fun things we can do without money. We could become greedy and piggy. We may even think we don't need God's help. Then who will want to be our friend?

Let's think about this a little more. If we could make our own friend, what kind of friend would really be best?

What did you say? I think you're right! Let's make a friend just like us.

Don't you think we will have lots and lots of fun together with this special new snow-friend? I do.

A Ride on My Sled

Will you go for a ride on my bright new
    sled?
  You'll like it, I guarantee.
We'll glide like a ship with wind-filled sails,
    in snowy woods on winding trails.
We'll laugh and sing about everything,
    as we ride, just you and me.

I'll ride with you on your bright new sled.
   I'll like it, I can see.
But I have a friend I must bring along,
   perhaps she'll help, she's really strong.
We'll laugh and sing about everything,
   just you and me . . . and she.

Will you go for a ride on my bright new
     sled?
   I guess it's okay for three.
We'll sail like a plane among clouds of
     snow,
   going wherever we want to go.
We'll laugh and sing about everything,
   just you and me . . . and she.

I'll ride with you on your bright new sled.
   I'm glad there's room for three.
But if three is okay, what about four?
   I know you won't mind if I bring some
     more.
We'll laugh and sing about everything,
   as they ride with you and me.

Will you go for a ride on my bright new
     sled?

It will be crowded, I can see.
But tell your friends to come along
and bring with them a happy song.
We'll laugh and sing about everything,
our friends and you and me.

February

A Heart Fixer-Upper

No one cared when her friends teased
    her,
    when one of them said,
    "I am not your friend!"
That's what Jennifer thought
    when she cried at school.
She was sure that her friends
    weren't friends at all.

Jennifer thought her heart would break.
She needed someone,
a heart fixer-upper,
for her heart felt like it was cut or bruised.

No one cared when a bully
got mean,
when he picked on a
little kid
who couldn't fight back.
That's what Jennifer
thought
when she cried at
school.
She was sure
there was no one
to make things right.
She felt that her heart was hurting inside.
Jennifer needed someone,
a heart fixer-upper,
for her heart felt like it was cut or bruised.

No one cared when her best friend cried,
when she said that her dad had run away.
That's what Jennifer thought
when she cried at school.

She was sure that no one
could help her friend.
She felt there was no one
who hurt for her friend.
Jennifer needed someone,
a heart fixer-upper,
for her heart felt like it was cut or bruised.

No one cared when
her brother wouldn't play,
when Mom and Dad were too busy.
That's what Jennifer thought
when she cried at home.
She was sure that no one knew
the pain she felt.
She thought that other things
were much more important.
Jennifer needed someone,
a heart fixer-upper,
for her heart felt like it was
cut or bruised.

No one cared when her
kitty got sick,

when she stayed up late
        to watch over her.
That's what Jennifer thought
        when she cried at home.
She was sure that no one knew
        how lonely she felt.
She thought that other things
        always came first.
Jennifer needed someone,
                a heart fixer-upper,
for her heart felt like it was cut or bruised.

Then Jennifer told a wise friend,
                a heart fixer-upper.
He brought his first-aid kit
        and he heard what her heart was
        saying.
He saw that it was hurt
        and needed to be fixed.
"I have a prescription," he said to Jennifer.
So he wrote his prescription
        on a little piece of paper.
Now that Jennifer knew
        someone else cared
when her heart felt cut or bruised,

233

she could follow his prescription
    to help her hurting heart.

This prescription sent Jennifer
    to see her mother.
And it said she should tell Mother
    exactly how she felt.
Mother listened to Jennifer
    and knew her heart was hurting.

And do you know
    what happened that day?
Mother said some special words
    that helped her broken heart.
And she put her arms around Jennifer
    and hugged her tight.
Then Jennifer knew
    that someone else cared.

She had found
        another fixer-upper
        to help her heart,
for Mother healed her heart
    from feeling cut and bruised.

"I have a prescription also,"
      Mother said to Jennifer.
Then she wrote it down
            on a little piece of paper.
      Then Jennifer did what this
      new prescription said.
            She went to her room
                  and began to pray.
            She talked with God
            and told him how she
            felt.

            Jennifer knew for sure
            that Someone else
                  cared.
            She knew that she
                  had found
            a special Someone,
            another fixer-upper
            who would always
                  help her heart.
            God healed her heart
                  from feeling cut
                  and bruised.

A Dozen or More Hearts

"I'll make a valentine for Dad," said Laura, on February 14. "He's a special dad, so I want to make a valentine that tells him how special he really is."

Laura found red construction paper. She found scissors and a pen. She brought all these things to the dinette table and sat down to work.

Laura smiled as she cut the construction paper into a big red heart.

"Wait until Dad sees this!" she said. She could see him now in her mind. He would be so happy when he read what she would write on this heart.

But what should she write?

"I know," said Laura. "I will write what I like best about him. But what do I like best about Dad?"

Laura began to think. "Dad plays games with me," she said. "That's special. He also takes me on trips. And he reads to me."

Laura kept on thinking about things she liked best about Dad. Soon she had a long list. She did not have just one thing she liked best about Dad. She had fourteen.

"That's a dozen!" Laura whispered. "No! That's more than a dozen! I can't write all of these things on this one heart."

Laura read the list again. Which one special thing did she want to write on the heart?

But they were all special. She really liked every one of these things about Dad. She liked each one as much as the others. How could she choose only one from the dozen or more special things?

Then Laura had a good idea. She began to cut more red hearts from the construction paper. Before long she had fourteen red hearts.

Laura wrote one special message on each heart. Each one told Dad something she liked best about him.

Laura strung the fourteen hearts on a long string. Just as she finished, her father walked into the room.

"Having fun?" he asked.

"Happy Valentine's Day!" said Laura. Then she gave her dozen or more hearts to Dad.

Don't you think Dad had fun reading what Laura wrote on those dozen or more hearts?

I
Don't Know
What
to Say

I want to write a little note
    to a very special person.
        But I don't know what to say.

I want to tell this special person
how very special she is.
But I don't know what to say.

I want to tell this special person
how thankful I am that she washes
my clothes and irons them.
But I don't know what to say.

I want to tell this special person
    how much I appreciate all the good
    meals she cooks for me.
        But I don't know what to say.

I want to tell this special person
    how much fun it is when we go shop-
    ping or do things together.
        But I don't know what to say.

I want to tell this special person
    how glad I am that she comes
    to all my school programs and things.
        But I don't know what to say.

I want to tell this special person
    that she has given me so many
    things and I just want to say some-
    thing wonderful about her.
        But I don't know what to say.

I want to say a hundred thank yous
    and a thousand nice things
    to this special person.
        But I don't know what to say.

I want to tell this special person
    that I want to be just like her
    when I grow up.
        But I don't know what to say.

I guess you know by now
    that I'm talking about you,
        Mother dear.
Would it be okay if I just tell you that
    I LOVE YOU
        today, Valentine's Day,
            and every other day too?

March

The Seas of Wind

Christopher watched the clouds in the
sky,
riding like ships on the seas of wind.
They were puffy white ships, sailing up
high,
looking for adventure on the seas of
wind.

"Where are you going?" Christopher
    called to them.
"Where are you headed on the seas of
    wind?"
  But the cloud ship captains
  were silent that day.
No one would whisper where they were
    going.
No one would tell why they were sailing.
No one would send
  one word for an answer.

The cloud ships were sailing
  on a great adventure.
They were looking for excitement
  on the seas of wind.

But where they were going was a secret.
No one would know,
  not even Christopher.
  Not even Christopher
    would know their secret,
    though he watched so carefully.

Not even Christopher
  would know
    where they were sailing.

They were sailing in silence
   on the seas of wind.
They were sailing in silence, so far away.

"Do these ships have captains?"
   Christopher whispered to himself.
"Is there someone to guide them
   on the great adventure?
Is there someone to guide them
   on the seas of wind?"

Soon Christopher sailed
   his kite in the sky.
   It sailed like a ship on the seas of wind.
It was a bright-colored ship,
   sailing that day on a great adventure.
"Up to the clouds," Christopher commanded.

Then he let out more string
   and the ship sailed higher,
   up and away on the seas of wind.

"Stop for a while!"
   Christopher commanded.

Then he tugged on the string
    and the bright-colored ship
        dropped anchor into
        the seas of wind.

"Come this way,"
    Captain Chris commanded.
When he pulled on the string,
    the ship sailed toward him.
It sailed on command
    of its earthbound captain
As it sailed that day
    on the seas of wind.

Christopher looked at the string
        in his hand.
He looked again at the kite in the sky,
    the bright-colored ship
        on the seas of wind.

He was captain of this ship
and he commanded its path.
    With a string he
showed it where to go
    sailing on the seas of wind.

So he held his string tightly
    and sent his ship sailing.
It could almost touch a white puffy cloud.
Could the two ships meet
    on the seas of wind,
    the bright-colored ship
        commanded by Christopher
    and the white puffy cloud ship
        on its great sea adventure?

Christopher watched
    as the clouds sailed away,
sailing like ships
    on the seas of wind.

The puffy white clouds,
    sailing that day,
were looking for adventure
    in a land far away.
Then he looked at his bright kite
    on the same windy seas,
sailing like a ship and looking
    for adventure.

He looked at the string,
    one end in his hand,
        the other stretching to the kite.

He watched
    as he guided his little kite ship,
    sailing away
        on the seas of wind.

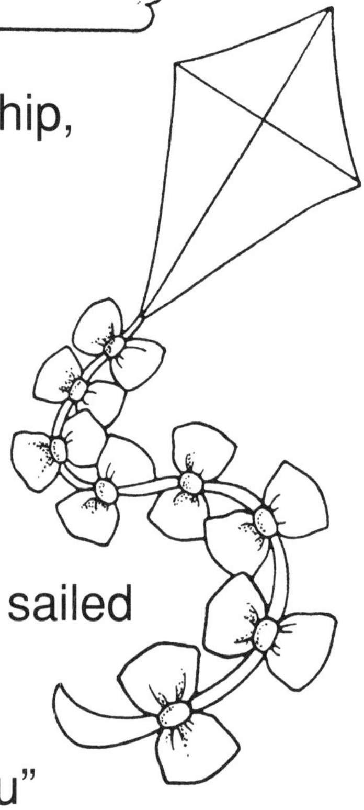

"The puffy white cloud ships
    have a Captain, too,
a Captain to guide them
    on the seas of wind,"
Christopher said as the ships sailed
    above him.

Then he whispered "thank you"
    to the unseen Captain,
he whispered a prayer
    for guiding these ships.
And he also said "thanks"
    for guiding him too,
as he dreamed of adventures
    on the seas of wind.

I'm Looking for a Friend

I'm looking for a friend today,
   A friend who'll never stay away.
I want one friend, or maybe two,
   But I want a friend who's just like you.

I'm looking for a friend, you see,
A friend who needs someone like me.

I want this friend, I really do,
But I want a friend who's just like you.

I'm looking for a friend sincere,
A friend who'll always bring good cheer.
I want a friend who wants me too,
But I want a friend who's just like you.

I'm looking for a friend who's good,
Who'll do the things a kind friend
should.
I want a friend who's happy too,
But I want a friend who's just like you.

I'm looking for a loving friend,
Who will not let our friendship end.
I want a friend who's always true,
I think I've found my friend—IT'S YOU!

Nobody Loves Me!

Have you ever said what Little Lamb said
When he stumbled and fell and banged
up his head?
"Nobody loves me!" that's what he said.
Then he cried when he felt the big knot
on his head.

"Nobody loves me! Nobody cares!"
Little Lamb grumbled when he tumbled
downstairs.
Later he stumbled over a root,
And a very sharp thorn stuck in his foot.

Before he could cry, a gaggle of geese
Honked and chased him and pecked at
his fleece.
And then a big bull, an obnoxious fellow,
Bellowed a horrendous, earthshaking
bellow.

This bull chased the lamb, snorting and
     puffing,
  Till it looked like he'd knock out the
     scared lamb's stuffing.
So now don't you know, now don't you
     see
  Why Little Lamb said, "Nobody loves
     me"?

I'm sure you'll admit, I'm sure you'll agree
  That Lamb had a right to say, "No one
     loves me!"
And maybe, just maybe, that's what you'll
     say
  When you get into trouble sometime
     later today.

But look! There is someone who heard
     the lamb say
  What he said when his troubles fell on
     him today.
Now what do you think that poor lamb will
     do
  When the shepherd says softly, "I love
     you!"

Do you ever cry, "Nobody loves me"?
And you sob so hard you can't even
see?
Whenever you do, I hope you will say,
"There's a Shepherd beside me who
loves me each day."

April

Sunshine and Raindrops

"I'm tired of snow," said Amy. "I wish it would never snow again."

"Never?" asked Father. "That's a long time. Do you remember the fun things you did in the snow this winter?"

Amy thought about the winter snow. "I really did have fun sliding down the hill on my sled," she said. "And we made this neat snowman and threw snowballs."

"And we counted snowflakes on your coat," said Father.

"I guess I really do like snow," said Amy. "But now I just want the sun to shine all the time."

"Always?" asked Father. "That's a lot of time for the sun to shine."

The next day Amy got her wish. The spring sun began to shine. Amy ran outside to play. She had so much fun playing outside. The sunshine was so nice and warm.

The sun shined all day. It shined all the next day too. And it shined for many days after that. Amy grew tired of nothing but bright sunshine.

"I guess I really don't want the sun to shine all the time," said Amy. "It would be nice to have some April showers. Then I could use my new umbrella. I wish it would rain all the time now."

"All the time?" asked Father. "That's a lot

of rain. But you do have a nice umbrella. I know you will have fun with it."

The next day Amy got her wish. Dark clouds raced across the sky. Raindrops began to fall. Amy was so happy. She ran outside with her new umbrella. She had so much fun. Her umbrella kept her quite dry while she watched the raindrops splash in the puddles. But of course she couldn't stay outside in the rain all day, could she?

It rained all that day. It also rained all the next day. Then it rained every day for several days.

"I'm tired of all this rain," said Amy finally. "I wish it would do something else. I wish it would never rain again. I would rather have snow than all this rain."

Father smiled. "But you said you never wanted snow again," said Father.

Amy looked up at Father. "I did say that, didn't I?" she said.

"You also said you would like sunshine all the time and rain all the time," Father said with a chuckle. "Or did you say you wished that it would never rain again? Would you

rather have sunshine all the time—or not at all? Or would you rather have raindrops always—or not at all?"

"What if we had a little of each?" Amy asked. "That would be better than always or never."

"So what would you like God to send now?" Father asked.

"Sunshine and raindrops," said Amy.

"Always or never?" Father asked.

"Whatever he thinks is best," said Amy.

Where Do Raindrops Come From?

Where do raindrops come from?
What is there way up high?
Does God have a garden hose
Sprinkling the April sky?

Where does lightning come from?
What is God trying to see?
Does he have a super flashlight
That he shines on you and me?

Where does thunder come from?
And why is it so loud?
Does God have a giant bowling ball
That he rolls from cloud to cloud?

Where do storm clouds come from
That bring us April rain?
Are these the shepherd's woolly sheep
That he sends past my window pane?

The Perfect Birthday Cake

"Happy birthday, Mother," said Jerry. "I'm going to make the perfect cake for you today." He imagined the yummy looking cake he would give her.

Mother smiled when she heard that. Would your mother smile if you said you were going to make a perfect birthday cake for her?

"What do you put into angel food cake?" Jerry asked.

"Do you want to make it from a cake mix or from scratch?" asked Mother.

Jerry wasn't sure what scratch was. But it sounded like it would make a more perfect cake than an old box mix.

"You'll need cake flour, baking powder, eggs, salt, sugar, and vanilla," said Mother. "May I help you?"

"No, thanks," said Jerry. "I want to do it all by myself."

Mother didn't say, "You can't do that." She didn't even say, "You shouldn't do that." She got out her favorite angel cake recipe and gave it to Jerry.

Then Mother quietly left the room.

Jerry whistled as he looked for the things to make the cake. When he found the flour and eggs he put them on the kitchen counter. Before long he also had sugar and salt and vanilla.

Jerry dumped some flour into a mixing bowl. He broke the eggs and dumped those into the flour. Then he poured in some vanilla and sprinkled a little bit of baking powder, some salt, and sugar into the bowl.

Jerry wondered how a perfect cake could come from such a gooey, lumpy mess. But he kept on whistling as he took a big spoon and stirred the gooey, lumpy mess as hard as he could. He stirred and stirred. Some of the lumps disappeared but it was still a gooey mess.

By this time Jerry wondered if maybe Mother shouldn't help him. But he still wanted to do it all by himself.

Jerry poured the gooey mess into a big cake pan. Then he popped the pan into the oven.

Just then Jerry's sister Terry came into the kitchen with their puppy FiFi.

"Whatcha doing?" she asked.

"Making a perfect birthday cake for Mother," said Jerry.

"Looks more like you're making a perfect mess," said Terry.

Jerry didn't think that was very funny. But he opened the oven door and showed Terry the cake. It certainly was a strange looking mess.

"Well, it doesn't look perfect to me," said Terry.

"Maybe it has baked too long," said Jerry. "It's been in there at least fifty minutes."

Jerry put on some padded gloves he had seen Mother use. Then he pulled out his perfect cake and dumped it onto a plate.

The cake sprawled into a mess on the plate. One side was done in spots, another

side sagged like it was too tired to stand up and be a cake. Jerry quickly stuck some birthday candles on the cake and showed it to FiFi. She thought it looked great. But Terry laughed.

"Yuk!" said Terry. "Is that a cake?"

Just then Mother walked into the kitchen. "Happy Birthday, Mother," said Jerry.

Mother almost laughed. But she didn't.

"I'm afraid it's not a perfect cake," said Jerry. "I'm afraid it's not even a good cake."

"Must be something wrong with the recipe," said Mother.

"Recipe?" said Jerry. "Oh, no! I forgot to follow the recipe! That's why it's a mess."

"I guess that's what happens to our lives when we forget to follow what God tells us, isn't it?" Terry asked.

"That's right," said Mother. "Maybe this isn't a perfect birthday cake. But I think it's a good reminder. When we think about this cake we'll remember that we need to follow a recipe or directions. It will help us remember to do exactly what God tells us. This certainly is a very special cake after all!"

May

Why Is
a Bee
Called
a Bee?

Why is a bee called a bee?
Why isn't it called a cee?
You can't be a bee,
   but you could see a cee,
so why don't we call it a cee?

Why is a bee called a bee?
Why isn't it called a dee?
Then we'd have bumble dees
   and honey dees.
How confusing to call a bee dee!

Why is a bee called a bee?
Why isn't it called an eee?
If a bee goes B-uzz
   would an eee go E-uzz?
Is that why it's not called an eee?

Why is a bee called a bee?
Why isn't it called a pea?
If bees were called peas,
   would peas be called bees?
Then Mother would say, "Eat your bees."

Why is a bee called a bee?
Why isn't it called a zee?
Would the honey we eat
   just put us to sleep
if it came from honey bee zzzs?

So why is a bee called a bee?
Would you rather it be cee, dee, or eee?
If you really don't mind, I think you will
    find
that it's better to let the bee be!

Why Doesn't This Thing Work?

When spring comes we think of our gardens and lawns. Do people at your house do that? They do at the house where Kenny and Kathy live.

One day Kenny took the garden hose from the garage. He tightened one end onto the faucet on the side of the house. Then Kenny picked up the other end of the garden hose. He pointed it at the flower bed and waited. But nothing came out.

"Why doesn't this thing work?" Kenny asked. He looked at the end of the hose. There was nothing in it to keep the water from coming out.

"We have to turn it on!" Kathy laughed. Kenny was still looking down into the end of the hose when Kathy turned the water on. What surprise do you think Kenny got?

Then Kathy and Kenny took the lawnmower from the garage. Kenny pulled on the starter rope. The lawnmower groaned and grunted. But it wouldn't start. Kenny pulled and pulled until he was too tired to pull anymore. But the lawnmower still would not start.

"Why doesn't this thing work?" Kenny wondered.

"Maybe we need a new lawnmower," said Kathy.

"Maybe we need gas in the tank," said Kenny. "I forgot to put gas in it." After Kenny filled it with gas he pulled the starter rope again. The lawnmower grunted once or twice. Then it started. Kenny mowed the lawn. That's what lawnmowers are for, aren't they?

Kathy took the electric grass clippers from the garage. She wanted to trim the grass along the sidewalk. Kathy carried the clippers to the sidewalk. She clicked the starter switch. But nothing happened. The clippers didn't move. They didn't even wiggle.

"Maybe we need new clippers," said Kenny.

"Maybe we need to plug the cord into the electric outlet," said Kathy. "I forgot to do that. Electric clippers won't clip if they are not plugged in, will they?"

Kathy plugged the end of the cord into the outlet. Then she clicked the starter switch. They worked! So Kathy neatly clipped the grass along the sidewalk.

That night at dinner Kathy and Kenny laughed about the things that didn't work.

They told Mother and Father about the hose that wouldn't give them water. They talked about the lawnmower that wouldn't mow. And they talked about the clippers that wouldn't clip.

"Many people are like that," said Father. "They want God to help them do things. But they don't even talk with him about these things. They don't remember to pray."

"Is prayer something like turning on the water, or filling a tank with gas, or plugging in an electric cord?" asked Kathy.

"If we want God's help, we have to turn it on or fill it up or plug it in," said Father. "That's what happens when we pray. Prayer makes lots of things work for us."

"I never thought of prayer that way," said Kenny.

"Neither have I," said Kathy.

Have you?

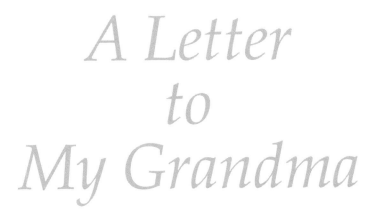

*A Letter
to
My Grandma*

Dear Grandma,
The other day a friend asked me,
"What's a grandma like?"

I guess you know by now,
That my friend didn't have one,
Or she wouldn't ask such things.
I tried to tell her a little
About what a grandma is like.
But it's hard to tell
Something special like that in words.

This is what I told her . . .
A grandma is a lot like a mom,
Except her lap is a little softer
And maybe there's a little more of it.

She always has a cookie for me
In her cookie jar,
And a quarter for me
In her purse.

Grandma likes to sing to me
And read to me,
Almost as much as she
Likes to play with me.

When I have breakfast
At Grandma's house,
She always asks me,
"What would you like to eat?"
And that's what we eat!

Grandma likes to shop with me
And I like to shop with her
Because she almost always
Buys me something I want.

My mother says
    Grandma spoils me.
But I think
    she just loves me.

When I go to bed at night,
I know that Grandma prays for me.

I'm glad you're my grandma.
There's no one quite like you
In all the world.
Thanks, Grandma, for being my grandma.

I know it's Mother's Day,
But I also want to say,
"Happy Grandmother's Day!
I love you."

Me.

Planting Seeds

This week Mother and I planted seeds. I had thought there was only one way to plant seeds. But I found that there are many kinds of seeds and many ways to plant them.

On Monday we took rakes, hoes, packets of seeds, and fertilizer to the garden. We dug up the dirt and raked it until it was soft. It was fun to put the little seeds into the furrows we dug. We mixed fertilizer into the dirt and covered the seeds with the soft dirt.

Mother said clouds will drop rain on our seeds. And the sun will shine on the dirt and keep it warm. Soon little green sprouts will peek out of the ground. They will grow into tall, strong plants.

Bean plants will grow from the bean seeds. Radishes will grow from the radish seeds. Beets will grow from those strange little beet seeds. That's the way God planned for new plants to grow.

You should have seen Mother and me when we finished. We had sweat running down our faces. And we had lots of dirt on our hands.

On Tuesday, my sister went for a walk with us to a beautiful meadow. It had lots of dandelions everywhere. Some had yellow flowers but some were like little white, fluffy balls.

Sis picked a fluffy white dandelion ball. She blew on it. Hundreds of little seeds came out and sailed away on the wind. Sis thought this was fun. She picked another

fluffy white dandelion and blew on it. More little seeds came out. They sailed away on the wind also. Sis blew on many dandelion seed balls. You should have seen her!

Mother said that Sis was planting seeds, too. She was planting dandelion seeds. But Sis did not have to dig up dirt. She did not have to make furrows. She did not have to get dirty or mix in some fertilizer. God planned for dandelion seeds to be carried by the wind. He helps them plant themselves when they fall to the ground.

On Wednesday Mother read a Bible story to me. She told me how God does special things in the lives of his people. And she told me how God can do special things in my life, too.

Mother said she is planting seeds whenever she reads the Bible to me or my sister. She said God will help good things to grow in us because we have heard God's truth from his Word. She said that's the way God planned for his truth to grow in people.

Mother doesn't have to dig up dirt to plant God's truth seeds in me. All she has to do is read something from the Bible or pray with me. God helps his truth seeds to grow beautiful things in me. He also helps his truth seeds grow good things in you.

Aren't you glad that God planned for some seeds to fly with the wind and garden seeds to grow to give us good food? And aren't you glad he planned for his truth seeds to grow in us, too?

June

Number One

Mother knew that Joey was sad when he came home from school. Mothers always seem to know those kinds of things.

"Bad day at school?" she asked.

"We played softball today at school," said Joey, softly. "I was chosen *last* for our team. I didn't hit the ball once. And I made two really bad errors. I guess I'm just not very good."

"Very good what?" asked Mother.

"Very good anything," said Joey.

"You may not be as good as some others when you're playing softball," said Mother. "But Father and I think you're in first place. When I ask you to clean your room, you're number one. When your sister needs a friend, you're number one. You're number one in many ways."

Mother smiled one of her I've-got-a-good-idea smiles. She took a large blue button, some blue ribbon, a little piece of red ribbon and a yellow "1." Soon she had a special award for Joey. She pinned it on him. "When Father comes home, he'll see that you're in first place," she said.

What do you think Joey did when he heard Father open the door?

Mary's mother knew that she wasn't on top of the world when she came home from school.

"Tell me about it," said Mother.

"Tell you about what?" asked Mary.

"About the not-so-good things that happened today at school," said Mother.

Mary knew that Mother knew more than Mary thought she knew. Mothers are like that, aren't they?

"My friends were not good friends today," said Mary. "Judy made fun of my dress. Sally laughed at me for getting a bad grade on my paper. And Terry said I'm a loser because she got the part I wanted in the school play."

"I'm sorry that my number-one-daughter wasn't number one with her friends today," said Mother. "But you're still number one with Father and me. When it's time to set the table, you're a number-one-helper. When kitty needs someone to take care of her, you're a number-one-friend. And when it's time for you to pray, you have a number-one-heart. Father and I think you are number one in many ways."

Mother hugged Mary tightly. Then she said, "I'm going to give you a special gift so you can look at it when you're feeling sad."

Mary's eyes sparkled when Mother handed her a pretty vase with a big "1st" on it.

"When Father comes home, you can show him you're in first place!" said Mother.

What do you think Mary did when she heard Father open the door?

It's
Much More Fun
with You

I want to go canoeing
   In my little birch canoe.
But canoeing is no fun alone;
   It's much more fun with you.

303

I want to have a picnic
  With a picnic lunch for two.
But a picnic is no fun to eat,
  Unless I eat with you.

I want to hike outside tonight
  And hear an owl go "whoo."
But hiking can be quite scary
  Unless I'm there with you.

I like to hear a story
  Of a tale that's old or new.
But what's the fun of hearing one
  Unless it's shared with you?

I like to pray at bedtime
  I know that you do, too.
So remember when *you* pray tonight
  That *I* will pray for you.

When
I
Become
a Man

"What will you do when you grow up?"
his aunt asked Danny today.
"What will you do and what will you be?

It's time to think and it's time to plan.
It's time to think about becoming a man.

Danny thought about what his aunt said.
He thought as he went for a walk
    through town.
"What will I do? How do I know?
But it's time to think and it's time to plan.
I really must know before I become a
        man."

When Danny came to Fourth and Main,
  he saw a policeman standing there.
He looked tall and straight with his uni-
    form.
So Danny thought about a possible plan.
"Perhaps I can be a policeman
  when I become a man."

Then a fire engine roared out
  the firehouse door.
Sirens whined and firemen waved.
They looked so brave as they rode along.
So Danny thought about
  another possible plan.
"Perhaps I can be a fireman
  when I become a man."

Danny thought he liked that plan
  until a pilot hurried by.
He was going to the airport
  where he would fly.
Perhaps he would fly a big plane around
    the world.
So Danny thought again
  about a possible plan.

"Perhaps I can be a pilot
  when I become a man."

But there were more. There were many
    more.
Danny saw them all as he stood by a
    store.
There were lawyers and doctors
  and milkmen, too.
Each time Danny wondered
  what he should do.
Each time he thought about a possible
    plan.
"Perhaps I can be that
  when I become a man.

"Should I be a soldier or sailor then?
Should I work in an office or run a bank?
Should I make tall buildings?
  What should I do?"
Each time he thought about a possible
    plan
  and thought he could do that
    when he became a man.

Danny was still thinking hard
  when he came back home.

He thought of policemen and firemen, too.
He thought of all the men
    he had seen that day.
And he thought of each possible plan
    and wondered what he would be
        when he became a man.

Then Danny saw his father sitting there.
He was sitting with his Bible
    in his favorite chair.
He knew what a great dad
                his dad had been.
                Then Danny thought of
                    a super great plan.
                "I want to be just like
                        Dad
                    when I become a
                        man!"

A Letter
to
My Grandpa

Dear Grandpa,
The other day a friend asked me,
"What's a grandpa like?"

I guess you
     know by
     now,
That he didn't
     have one,
Or he wouldn't
     ask such
     things.

I tried to tell him a
     little
About what a
     grandpa is like.
But it's hard to tell
Something special
     like that in words.
This is what I told
     him . . .

A grandpa is a lot like a dad
Except he always spoils you
And never spanks you.
He has whiter hair than a dad,
But not as much of it.

A grandpa smiles like sunshine
And showers gifts like rain.
When I come to my grandpa's house,
I meet his arms first,
Then the rest of him.
He gives big hugs
And little pieces of candy.
He always has time to play,
Even when I know he doesn't.

A grandpa asks me questions
About me.
He wants to know
What other people don't even care about,
And what makes me such a good boy.

A grandpa likes to say yes
And hates to say no.
When I'm with Grandpa,
I'm the most important person
In the world.
A king or prince
Would not get more
    of Grandpa's attention
Than I do.

When I go
to bed at night,
I know that
Grandpa
prays for me.

I'm glad you're my grandpa.
There's no one quite like you
In all the world.

Thanks, Grandpa, for being my grandpa.

I know it's Father's Day,
But I also want to say,
"Happy Grandfather's Day.

I love you."

Me.

July

This Warm Summer Day

"Where have you been
   on this warm summer day?"

"I went to find a gift for you."

"What did you find
   on this warm summer day?"

"I found a gift that says,
'I LOVE YOU.'"

The Best Parade Ever

It's no fun when your very best friend breaks his leg. Eric knew that it was no fun for Bobby to stay inside all day. And it was no fun for Eric either. He felt sorry because his friend was hurting.

Eric wondered what he could do to cheer his friend. What would you do if you were Eric? Eric knew that it had to be something special because Bobby was special. But what?

"Why don't I send a parade past his house?" Eric thought. "But it must be a big parade. It must be the very best parade ever."

Eric could see the parade in his mind. It would have elephants and zebras,

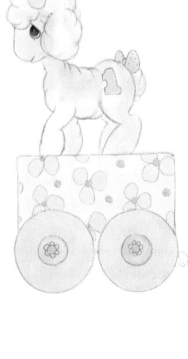

lions and giraffes, calliopes and organ grinders. And, of course, every parade must have lots of people playing music.

There would be horn-tooters and drum-beaters, whistle-blowers and baton twirlers. Nothing less than a dozen of each would do. Maybe two dozen of each would be better.

Before long, Eric's daydream parade was a mile long. Eric thought it might even become two miles long. But there was nothing too good for his friend with the broken leg.

Eric's parade was the most wonderful

parade ever. He had never seen a better parade than the one he saw in his mind.

Eric was so happy about his special parade. He jumped up and started to run. He would get his parade together now!

But suddenly Eric stopped. Where would he find all those things? Where would he get all the animals and musicians? Where would he find the calliopes and organ grinders?

Suddenly Eric felt sad. He knew that there wasn't one calliope in his town. There wasn't one organ grinder either. There wasn't one elephant or zebra or giraffe. There wasn't one thing that he needed for his parade.

Then Eric remembered something. There *was* one thing for the parade. Eric ran home as fast as he could. Before long, he was back at his friend's house.

Eric marched in front of Bobby's window. He beat on his drum. "Boom, BOOM, boom!" went Eric's drum. Bobby looked out the window. He smiled. There was his own special parade, with his own special friend.

There were no elephants or lions or zebras or giraffes. There were no horn-tooters or baton twirlers. There were no calliopes or organ grinders. But there was one VERY SPECIAL drum beater.

Don't you think Bobby was happy that day? He had the best parade ever because Eric was his very best friend, and Eric's parade was just for him. That really is quite special, isn't it?

A Family Is Fun

A family is fun, I think you'll agree,
whether the family is one, two, or three.
It really doesn't matter how many there
     are,
until you squeeze into the old family car.

There's a puppy,
a hamster,
a goldfish or two,
a pigeon,
canary,
and stuffed kangaroo.

For a family is never a family yet
until it collects every imaginable pet.

A family is fun, I think you should know,
whether we're swimming or out in the
      snow.
We may be making a snowman or two
or cutting up paper or gluing with glue.
We'll go to the circus or stop at the store.
And whatever we do, we'll always do
      more.
We'll go to the park or visit the zoo.
We'll go on a picnic. Can you go, too?

A family is fun, a super success,
except when Sarah spilled ink on her
      dress.
And kitty fell into the bowl with our fish,
when puppy chased her away from his
      dish.
Then Randy and Sandy got into a fight,
'cause each thought the other
    just couldn't be right.

A family is fun, as anyone knows
who has trimmed and scrubbed
sixty-three dirty toes.

Sixty-three?
Could it be?
We miscounted tonight?
I know sixty-three just couldn't be right!
I'd better go back
    and count them once more.
Who knows—I may find
    that there are sixty-four!

A family is fun, a family is fine
until you must stand in the family bath
        line.
It's really no fun when Sis beats me there
and spends half the morning
    to blow dry her hair.

A family is fun, we dine like kings,
    on hamburgers,
    hot dogs,
    milkshakes,
    and things.
We get scratches
    and cuts,
    poison ivy
    and sneezes.

We share every sniffle
   and many diseases.

But a family is fun, that really is true.
We never run out of fun things to do.
Where else can you laugh
   and do things together,
in all kinds of places
   and all kinds of weather?
Where else can you have
   such wonderful friends?
It's one friendship
   that never, ever ends!

Yes, our family is great,
   I'm glad for each one in it
And I'm thankful that God
   is with us each minute.

August

What's on the Other Side?

Yesterday I looked into a hollow log. There was a big wide world on the other side. It looked like the world I live in. The bunny on the other side looked just like a bunny I saw near the log.

Do you suppose that place on the other

side of the hollow log is just like the place where I am? Maybe it is. If I'm happy here, I would probably be happy there. If I'm unhappy here, I would probably be unhappy there. If I grumble here, I would probably grumble there, too.

This morning I looked at the mirror in my room. There was someone on the other side of the mirror. And there was a room on the other side, too.

When I smiled, the girl in the mirror smiled back at me. When I moved back, she moved back, too. Mother said the girl on the other side of the mirror looks just like me. She must be my twin, or something like that. I guess she's a special person.

The room on the other side of the mirror looks just like my room. Do you suppose this special someone lives just the way I do in a room just like mine? I wonder what it would be like to live on the other side of my mirror. Mother said she thought it would be just like living here. If I like to have good friends here, I would probably like to have good friends there. If I don't obey here, I probably would not obey there.

This afternoon Mother wanted me to do some chores. I wanted to play. I grumbled and complained. I said something like, "I wish I didn't live here any more. Then I wouldn't have to do my old chores any more."

Mother smiled. "Would you rather live on the other side of the log?" she asked. "Or would you rather live on the other side of your mirror? You'd probably have the same chores there. And Mother there would also want you to do them."

Do you know what? I think Mother is right. And I think I would really rather stay on this side of the log. I'd rather stay on this side of my mirror, too. Wouldn't you?

Do You Ever Make Mistakes?

Do you ever make mistakes? I do. Some of them are little mistakes. Some of them are not so little.

But what do you do when you make a mistake? I'll tell you what I do. Sometimes I say that my brother did it. That's not very nice, is it? At other times I say that kitty or puppy must have done it.

And sometimes I have to say that I did it. But it wasn't my fault. That crazy car just hit the meter all by itself. Do you think anyone believes me when I say that? No, I guess not.

Sometimes I get angry when I make a mistake. Sometimes I cry. Sometimes I even scream. But none of these things really helps.

Do you know what I've found helps the most? When I make a mistake now, I try to pray. God knows I'm not perfect. He knows I may make another mistake tomorrow. But he forgives me. I'll forgive you when you make your next mistake.

I know my mistake made you very un-happy. I'm really VERY, VERY sorry. I hope you'll forgive me now. So thank you for forgiving me. You will, won't you?

Here
Can Be
Better
Than
There

George Gimme Getaway Gare
wants to go somewhere,
but doesn't know where.
He wants to go anywhere
as long as it's not here,
and that, I suppose,
must be somewhere out there.

George wants to be someone he's not,
　　and he's really quite tired
　　　　of all he's now got.

George is bored with everything Here,
　　and that is why he wants to be There.
Yes, There is the place
　　　George wants to go,
　　though what is There he doesn't know.

George doesn't care about what is There
　　as long as he gets away from Here.
What's wrong with Here?
　　　It's what he's now got.
And he's more concerned
　　with what he has not.

George is packed and ready for There,
　　though he's found that There
　　　can be anywhere.
It can be any place that isn't Here.
　　　So how can he go just anywhere?
　　　How will he know
　　　when he's really There?

Now you see the problem
    that George has got.
It's the problem of wanting
    to go where he's not.
It's the problem of trying
    to leave what he's got.
It's the problem of trying
    to be someone he's not.

George Gimme Getaway Gare
    lives down your street,
    almost anywhere.
He's a kid on your block
    or a kid next door,
almost any kid
    who thinks he wants more.

George is a kid like us kids everywhere.
    We have everything Here
    but wish we were There.

I hope you will talk with
    George G. G. Gare
    before he leaves Here
    and tries to go There.

When George gets There,
He will wish he were Here,
For Here looks the best
    when you finally get There.

Do you ever wish
    you were somewhere you're not,
    or someone you're not?

Ask G. G. G. Gare what you've got.
You've got a lot!

Don't wish what you haven't
    instead of what you've got,
for something out There
    that maybe is not.
For if you were There
    with what is not,
you'd wish you were Here
    with all you've now got.

Are you thankful, quite thankful,
    for what you've now got?
Would you like to thank Someone
    right Here on the spot?

September

There's a Worm in My Apple

Summer was over for Eddie McGee.
  It was back to school on September 3.
It was back to school on a sunny day—
  when he'd rather, much rather,
    stay home to play.
He tried to think of some kind of rule
  that would help him stay home
    and not go to school.

Ed had an excuse, in fact he had four.
   But Mother had heard each one before.
So Ed McGee started again
   to engineer a better plan.
But you'd have to be smart,
   you really would,
   to outsmart Mom,
      who knows what's good.

You know how Ed feels,
     I know that you do.
When school days begin,
     you'd rather play, too.
You dread doing math and so you act sick.
You develop fake sneezes
     with imaginary diseases.

But Mom knows your game
     she certainly does.
Whatever you plan, it already was.
And every time you try a new scheme,
     she knows that the scheme
          is only a dream.
So you may as well plan
     on school the first day.
That's what I think your mother will say.

Now teachers like apples,
     that's what Mom said.
And she told Ed to take one
     that's bright shiny red.
But Ed was still feeling
     quite grumpy and snide,
so he chose a bad apple
     with a worm inside.

But somewhere on his way to school
    Ed remembered a verse called
        The Golden Rule.
He thought what he'd want if he were she.
He wouldn't want worms from Eddie
        McGee.
He'd not want an apple that's sure to of-
        fend,
but one that would say,
        "I'm your new friend."

So Ed junked the apple,
    the one with the worm,
    that would make his teacher
        shriek and squirm.
And he got another one fit for a queen
    and washed it
    and wiped it
        all squeaky clean.

Then Ed was glad
    he remembered that Rule.
He was even glad now
    to go back to school.

349

If You Love Me

If you love me—
Will you give me
Everything I ask
    of you?

If I love you—
I will give you
Only what is best
    For you.

If you love me—
You won't hurt me,
Not the smallest hurt
    Will do.

If I love you—
I must hurt you
When the hurt
    Is best for you.

An Un-bearable Ouchy

Have you never a care
  like Timothy Bear,
    who thought he was quite lucky?
Until one day
  he was heard to say,
    "I'm beginning to feel quite yukky."

When Tim reached the nurse
he was feeling much worse.
He was grumbly and gritchy and grouchy.
But the nurse put Tim Bear
up on her small chair,
and gave him one more ouchy.

"Don't you care?
Don't you see,
that your shot has hurt me?
It really made me yelp."
But the nurse said to Bear,
"Yes, I really do care,
and my shot is the way to help."

Sometimes folks give us shots
or other whatnots
and we wonder why they do.
But if these hurts help
we should not yelp,
because they say, "I love you."

Flying High

Once there was a boy named Alan who liked to walk outside and think about God. Every time he saw a cloud he thought about the wonderful things that God had made. Alan often sat down on the green grass and looked up into the sky.

Sometimes he saw clouds shaped like animals. One big cloud looked like an elephant. A much smaller cloud was like a little lamb. There were many other cloud animals in the sky, too. Alan knew that God made each cloud. He wanted to find a way to get closer to God. If he could ride on one of those clouds, would that help him get closer to God?

At other times Alan climbed into a tree. He felt the rough bark and listened to the wind sighing among the leaves. In September he might see an acorn or an apple hanging from a branch while the leaves drifted down. Alan knew that God made all these things

grow. He wanted to find a way to get closer to God. If he could climb to the top of the highest tree in the world, would that help him get closer to God?

Alan liked to climb up on a high hill near his home. He looked at the houses and fences and fields below. He could see far away. He could see many things. He knew that God had made every living thing that he saw—all the plants and animals and people down below. The boy wanted to find a way to get closer to God. If he could climb up on the highest hill in the world, would that help him get closer to God?

Alan talked with his friends about these things—about the clouds, the trees, and the high hills. He told them how he wanted to find a way to get closer to God. He asked them which way they thought was best.

One friend said, "There is no God." Another friend said, "There is a God. But why bother to get closer to him? He probably doesn't care about us anyway." A third friend said he thought it was a good idea to get closer to God because God really does care about us. But he also said that clouds and trees and hills are not high enough. He said Alan should fly high into the sky. That would help him get closest to God.

So Alan sat down and began to think about flying. He pretended to make a special little plane. He even gave it a special name, "Heaven Bound." In his mind he pretended to fly this plane far above the clouds. He went higher and higher until he thought he must be flying near the front door of heaven. But Alan did not feel any closer to God up there than he did down below on the ground.

That night Alan talked with his father about all these things. He asked his father

why he did not seem closer to God in his
little plane.

Alan's dad smiled. He told Alan that God
is not "up there" somewhere. He is "down
here" with us. God promised to be with us

each day. And he told Alan that the best way to get closer to God is to read his Book, the Bible, and talk with him often.

So Alan did exactly what his father had said. He read God's Book, the Bible. And he prayed.

Then he really and truly felt closer to God than he ever had before.

October

Jonathan C.

Jonathan C.,
   a big boy is he.
A very big boy is
   Jonathan C.
He's as big a boy
   as a boy could be.
That's how big is
   Jonathan C.

Jonathan C.,
   a very big boy is he.
He's so big
   all the team wants
Jonathan C.
   That's how big is
Jonathan C.

Jonathan C.,
   how big is he?
He's so big
   all the guys are afraid,
you see.
   That's how big is
Jonathan C.

Jonathan C.,
   what a man is he!
He's a man as much
   as a man can be.
That's how big is
   Jonathan C.

Jonathan C.
  is bigger than me
and I stretch up
  to an elephant's knee.
That's how big is
  Jonathan C.

Jonathan C.
  wants to play
with me,
  but I feel like a
     flea
  when he's
     with me.
That's how
  big is
  Jonathan
     C.

Jonathan C.
  is as big as three.
"All the pro teams want me,"
  says he.
That's how big is
  Jonathan C.

Jonathan C.,
  a giant is he.
No one's as big,
  I think you'll agree.
That's how big is
  Jonathan C.

Jonathan C.,
   how big is he?
"How big is BIG?"
asks Jonathan C.
   "That's how big is
Jonathan C."

So if you want to play
   with Jonathan C.,
   you'd better be big,
      as big as he.
You may want to bring
   your own referee,
      'cause there's a big boy, that
Jonathan C.

But now it's bedtime for
   Jonathan C.
It's time to sit on Mother's knee.
   "Tell me a story about God,"
      says he.
Now *there's* someone bigger than
   Jonathan C.

Little Mouse Under the Pumpkin Leaf

Little Mouse under the pumpkin leaf,
where will you sleep tonight?
Where is your house, and what is it
like?

Is there a kitchen with table and chairs?
Do you have carpets,
    perhaps an upstairs?
Is there a place for a welcome mat,
Welcoming all but the neighborhood
    cat?
Do you have a front door
    for friends that are new?
And a door in the back
    for old friends, too?

Little Mouse under the pumpkin leaf,
    where will you sleep tonight?
Where is your house and what is it like?

                Is there a place I can
                call and find what
                    is there on your table,
                or what there is not?
                    Will you have some
                tasty food there?
                    Do you have your own
                special chair?
                    Will dinner be served at
                your table tonight—

With napkins and spoons
　　and soft candlelight?

Little Mouse under the pumpkin leaf,
　　　where will you sleep tonight?
　　Where is your house and what is it like?
　　Do you have a soft bed to
　　　cuddle down in—
　　With covers to pull
　　　all the way to your chin?
　　Will your mother read stories
　　　and kiss you good-night?
　　Will you sleep by the light
　　　of a soft night light?
　　Do you sleep in your own
　　　room upstairs?
　　Do Mother and Dad have you say
　　　your own prayers?

Little Mouse under the pumpkin leaf,
　　　where will you sleep tonight?
　　Where is your house and what is it like?
　　Can anyone see your little house—
　　The house just right for a wee, tiny
　　　mouse?

Should I worry that no one
    will take care of you?
No, I won't worry. I know it is true,
That the Someone who sees
    the things I do,
Watches over a Little Mouse, too.

373

November

Thank You!

"Thank you for the wonderful turkey dinner," Michael said to his grandmother. It was always special to come to Grandmother's and Grandfather's farm for Thanksgiving Dinner.

"You are welcome," Grandmother said with a big smile. "But I'm not the only one who helped you have this wonderful turkey dinner."

Michael remembered that Mother had brought the vegetables. Aunt Ellen had brought the salad. Aunt Elizabeth had brought the dessert.

Michael thanked Aunt Ellen. He thanked Aunt Elizabeth. And he thanked Mother, too.

"I'm glad you are thankful," said Mother. "But there are others who helped us have this wonderful meal."

Michael thought about this. Then he remembered that Uncle Henry earned money to buy things for the dessert. Uncle Charles earned money to buy things for the salad. Father earned money to buy the vegetables. And Grandfather earned money to buy the turkey.

Michael thanked Uncle Henry. He thanked Uncle Charles. He thanked Grandfather. And he thanked Father.

"I'm glad you're thankful to us," said Fa-

ther. "You are a very thoughtful boy. But others helped us have this wonderful Thanksgiving Dinner. Do you know who?"

Michael tried to think of others. But he couldn't think of anyone else who had brought food or earned money to buy it.

"Let's start with the grocers who sold us all these things," said Father. "Grocers help us get good food from many different places."

"I'm thankful for the grocers," said Michael. "But where did the grocers get the food?"

Then Father and Michael thought about other people who helped them get their Thanksgiving Dinner. Michael thought about the farmers who raised the vegetables. He thought about the people who raised the turkey. He thought about the dairy farmer whose cows gave milk and cream for the ice cream.

"And how did all of these people get their food to the grocer?" asked Father.

Michael remembered the butchers who got the turkeys ready to sell. He thought of the people who drove the trucks and the engineers who ran the trains that hauled all the food. He thought of other people who handled it along the way.

Michael soon had a long list of people who helped them have a wonderful Thanksgiving Dinner. "I can't thank each of them in person," said Michael. "But I am thankful for each and every one."

"There's one more person you *can* thank,"

said Father. "He helped us have everything on the table and a lot more."

Michael thought for a long time. Then he remembered. "God gave us everything we ate," he said. "And I can thank him!"

Michael went outside where he could be alone. Do you know what he did out there?

I'm Thankful for Brushes and Brooms

I heard Mom say as she scrubbed today,
"I'm thankful for brushes and brooms.
I'm glad to clean my cozy house
That's filled with cheerful rooms."

I heard Mom say at the washing machine,
"I'm thankful for dirty clothes.
I'm glad that I have a healthy child
Who can play each day she grows."

I heard Mom say at the sink tonight,
"I'm thankful for dirty dishes.
I'm glad we filled our plates with food
Instead of empty wishes."

I heard Mom say in her prayers tonight,
"I'm thankful for problems today.
If life never got a little bit rough,
I might forget to pray."

Where Does Winter Come From?

Where does winter come from?
And where does summer go?
Who makes November's skies above
and icy fields below?

Where do snowflakes come from?
I really want to know.
Who will shape a million jewels
    into a drift of snow?

Where do autumn nuts come from?
Do flowers fly away—
into a kingdom far away,
    until a summer day?

Where do winter trees come from,
Which drop their summer leaves?
And where do autumn colors go
    before November's freeze?

Where do cold winds blow from?
And why are they like that?
Is it because God turns down low
    his weather thermostat?

Where do winter birds come from?
And where do summer ones fly?
Does someone guide them on their way
    on highways through the sky?

I know where winter comes from.
And where all summers go.
Each changing season comes from God.
    He made the sun and snow.

December

How Can I Make the Angels Sing?

How can I make the angels sing?
    What can I do or say?
If I help Mom and Dad
And try hard to obey,
Will that make the angels sing today?

How can I make the angels sing?
What can I do or say?
If I don't quarrel or fight
And am careful to do right,
Will that make
the angels
sing
today?

How can I
make the
angels
sing?
What
can I do
or say?
If I read in my
Bible
And I don't
forget to
pray,
Will that make
the angels
sing
today?

How can I make the angels sing?
　　　What can I do or say?
If I help a friend know Jesus
And show him Jesus' way,
Will that make the angels sing today?

A
Christmas Eve
Gift

The moon was bright on Christmas Eve
   as Jeremy walked in the snow.
He smiled up and the moon smiled down.
He wished he could talk
   with the man in the moon,
and share some Christmas secrets.

"I wonder what gifts I'll get tonight,"
Jeremy whispered to himself.
He thought of the list he had given to
    Dad,
  and the copy he had given to Mom.
His list was as long as a kangaroo's tail
  and he wanted everything on it.

There were gadgets and trinkets
	and a cuddly bear,
	and things to make and things to break.
There were candy canes and wind-up
	trains
	And things and things and things.
His list was as long as a kangaroo's tail
	and he wanted everything on it.

Each step he took made him think of a
	thing,
	and each thing was bigger than
	the thing before.
There were things enough
	to crowd his room.
And things enough to squeeze out the
	door.
Where, O where, would he put
	all these things?
His list was as long as a kangaroo's tail,
	and he wanted everything on it.

Jeremy thought the moon frowned
	as he thought of those things.
Though the frown of the moon made him
	frown a bit, too.

He couldn't stop thinking
    of his list of things.
He couldn't stop thinking
    of things he could make
    and things he could run
    and things he could hold.
Things and things, and things.
His list was as long as a kangaroo's tail
    and he wanted everything on it.

Each step Jeremy took
    said "crunch" in the snow.
He really wasn't sure
    which way he would go.
But he wanted to walk
    some more and think
    of each thing he had put on his list.
He was sure he would get
    every one, even more.
And the more he thought,
    the more he wished
he had asked for more things
    on his Christmas list.

But his list was already as long
    as a kangaroo's tail,
  and he wanted everything on it.

Then Jeremy stopped by a lamp
    on the street,
a lamp wrapped with holly and snow.
He stood and looked
    in the window nearby.
There he saw an old lady,
  a lady alone in the soft yellow light,
  a lady with no list and no one to love
    on Christmas Eve.

A tear came to Jeremy's eye that night.
The lady alone
    had no Christmas tree,
    no gifts in the corner
        wrapped in bright-colored paper,
    no wreaths or cones or candy canes.
    No children to sing and clap their
        hands,
    no laughter or feasting or fun.

What gift would she want?
And who would give it?
Then Jeremy thought
    of the gifts on his list,
    that list as long as a kangaroo's tail.
  And he wasn't so sure he wanted each
    one.

Then Jeremy had a wonderful thought.
He ran home through the snow,
    and up to his room.
In a wink and a twinkling
    he was back once again.
He was back at the lamp
    with the holly leaves.
He was back at the window
    with soft yellow light.
He was back near the lady
    with no gifts in sight.
He stood there with a book
    in his hands on that night.

Jeremy lifted his book with a smile.

And he sang a sweet song
       of the Christ Child's birth.
His song was a gift to the lady alone.
He smiled as he sang,
       and she smiled, too.
Then he knew that his gift
       was the best he could give.

In the snow that night,
       by the soft yellow light,
    Jeremy forgot the list he had made.
He forgot the list of things and things.
He was giving, not getting.
       He was singing, not taking.
       He was bringing a gift
               of himself and his song.
And that was the best gift
       on that Christmas Eve night.

There by the lamp as the snowflakes fell,
by the lamp with the holly leaves
       wrapped all around,
Jeremy sang his songs of love.

He sang many songs of a Savior's birth

and the joy he could bring to a lady
alone.
Jeremy had a long list of songs to sing.
His list was as long as a kangaroo's tail
and he sang for her *every* one.

Something
Different
for Christmas

Marsha giggled when she saw Andy playing in his room. It looked as if he was in a toy store. There were toys everywhere.

"You don't need any more toys for Christmas," said Marsha. "But what can I give you?"

"Something different," said Andy.

"Like what?" asked Marsha.

"Like something different from anything in this room," said Andy.

Just then Andy's dog Sandy looked into his room. "I suppose you'll ask what I want for Christmas, too," Andy grumbled at Sandy. Sandy just wagged his tail.

That night Marsha had a what-shall-we-get-Andy-for-Christmas meeting with Mother and Father. But no one knew what different gift Marsha could give him. "We'll just have to keep thinking about it, Marsha," Father said at last.

In the morning Marsha had a little talk with Sandy. Marsha did all the talking and Sandy wagged his tail. "I suppose you know exactly what to give Andy," she said. "I certainly don't."

Sandy wagged his tail again.

Then Marsha had a good idea. "Sandy, you and I will give Andy the most different gifts that he has ever had," she said. She could hardly wait until Christmas to give these different gifts to Andy.

On Christmas day Andy opened all his gifts. All but Marsha's gift. Where was that?

"Sandy and I have gifts for you outside," Marsha told Andy. "Come with us."

Andy put on his old coat and one of his Christmas hats and went with Marsha and Sandy. He was certainly surprised when Sandy gave Andy a bone with a ribbon on it. Then Andy saw a little note on the ribbon.

"My gift is the gift of Christmas happiness," said the note. "Give one of your special toys to a boy who doesn't have much. You will learn something about being happy." It was signed, "Sandy."

"Now let's go back in the house and put on the new coats and hats Grandma gave us," said Marsha. Andy didn't like to change clothes but this was Christmas and he was too happy to fuss over such a little chore.

"OK, now let's get my gift for you," said Marsha. She led Andy to a little ice cream stand.

"Usually I would charge you for this special snowball ice cream cone. But today it's free!" she said. "So is the Christmas note in the cone." When Andy ate the snowball, he found the little slip of paper in the cone.

"My gift is the gift of Christmas love," the note said. "Give one of your special toys to another boy who doesn't have much. You will learn something special about love." It was signed, "Marsha."

Andy thought about the two very different Christmas gifts. He thought about the Christ-

mas happiness note and the Christmas love note.

"I'll do it!" he said.

Andy wrapped two special toys in Christmas paper. As he did, he felt happier than he had all day. "That's my gift of Christmas happiness," he said.

Then Andy thought of two boys at school who wouldn't get much for Christmas. He would take his special toys to them right now. Suddenly Andy felt more love in his heart than he had all day. "That's my gift of Christmas love," he said.

Soon Andy was walking down the street with the special Christmas toys. He was sure Marsha and Sandy had given him the very best Christmas gifts ever. What do you think?